FLASH TALES 2

Includes 56 winners and runners-up
from the Web contest
(see www.FlashFiction5.com)
and 120 stories from the original 6
authors
of FLASH TALES

Edited and with an Introduction
by Janda Raker

Cover by Janda Raker
and Emma D at PhylissMiranda.com

*Dedicated to all
who love to read
and to write
—both long and short—
and all who support
those endeavors.*

FLASH TALES 2

TABLE OF CONTENTS

INTRODUCTION

If you are a fan of short stories and have just a minute to read--between all the busyness of your day--then flash fiction is perfect for you. This volume contains enough little tales to keep you entertained for many of those brief times—176 stories by 23 different authors!

Flash Tales 2 **is** the second anthology of flash fiction I've collected and edited. The first was called simply *Flash Tales,* published in December, 2009, by a small publisher in West Texas. It included 100 stories, 20 each by 5 writers. It is available through Amazon.com and BarnesandNoble.com.

Flash fiction is extremely short fiction, length decided by the author or editor--as short as fifty-five words and as long as two thousand words. Each must include all the elements of regular fiction—setting, characters, plot, conflict, and resolution, and most with a twist at the end.

The tales in these two volumes are different from most stories, in that they were produced from a formula or assignment—certain words, or a form of each word, were required to be used in each story. Writers were given five or six words to be included in their stories, and no tale could be over 100 words, plus the title. Each story can be read in less than a minute!

There are two separate sections of this book, with two different sets of authors--

The first section contains stories that were the winners and runners-up of a monthly contest conducted on our website, www.FlashFiction5.com . Each month, we post five new, random words on the website, and readers/writers from around the country use those words to create 100-word stories of their own and submit them through the website. The stories in that section were submitted from the contest's inception in January, 2010, through December, 2011, when we concluded the collection of stories for this anthology--although the contest continues. (If you're interested in creating little stories like this yourself, go online and give it a try.) Our judge receives the stories without authors' names and chooses a winner and a runner-up. The winning story is posted on the website for the following month, for readers to enjoy. So far, we've had contestants from Maryland, Utah, North Carolina, Pennsylvania, South Carolina, and Texas, from sixteen different cities.

The second section has 120 stories—of the same length and formula—written by six authors who were involved in the original *Flash Tales* book. We six writers had been members of a critique group that met each week to edit each other's writing. But we were not writing much, needed something to make us more productive. We decided to write a flash-fiction story every week, but we wanted a prompt to get us started. So we each wrote down a word at random, then shared our words, with a commitment to create a story using those words—or a form of the words--by the next week. We thought all the stories written from one list of words would be much alike. However, those stories were all quite different! After many months, we collected the stories and published the first anthology. That volume contained 100 tales because one of the original authors chose not to have her stories included. But we're happy she joined us in this volume--20 stories each, by 6 authors, a total of 120 stories, for readers to enjoy.

Besides accomplishing our **goal** of being more-productive writers, we realized **the advantage of learning to write "tight," without wasted words**. That skill has improved our writing in our many genres—including short stories, travel essays, poetry, thrillers, humor, devotionals, memoirs, and personal interviews. We're hoping the writers in the website contest and those who begin to write flash fiction as a result of reading this volume will also benefit from this discipline.

At the beginning of each section is a table of contents, with the title of each tale, the author's name, and the page number where that story may be found. After that is a page with all the lists of words for that section. We think readers will enjoy checking the word lists and perhaps writing their own stories using those words. A hint: it's much easier to write your own stories BEFORE you look at the stories by other authors!

And for each set of stories—two or more for the contest winners, six for the original authors—**the list of five words required for those stories is given at the beginning** of that set. So you, the reader, can see what words the authors had to use to create those stories. A fun aspect is seeing how different the stories are that used the SAME words. Those words are underlined in every story so the reader can see how the words are used by each author.

If you would like to get in touch with any of the authors from this volume, e-mail me at JandaRaker@gmail.com, and I'll give that author your contact information.

We hope you will enjoy reading these little tales as much as we did creating them. So if you have a minute now, turn to a story and **read**!

Janda Raker
Editor/Coauthor

TABLE OF CONTENTS
OF
CONTEST-WINNING STORIES AND AUTHORS--
WWW.FLASHFICTION5.COM

from January, 2010-December, 2011
in order by month, oldest first.

April, 2011--
1. tie for 1st -- *A Hand for a Tooth* -- Yvonne Byrd Nunn   46
2. tie for 1st -- *Lana and Jonathan* -- Pamela B. Kessler   46
3. tie for 2nd -- *True Crime* -- Elisha Cheeseman   47
4. tie for 2nd -- *In the Eye of the Beholder* -- Glenn Baldwin   48

May, 2011--
1. *Sometimes You Just Can't Win* -- Don W. Bonifay   49
2. *Nature's Way Is Best* -- Mart Baldwin   49

June, 2011--
1. *Do Superheroes Really Battle to Save Us?* -- Glenn Baldwin   50
2. *The Settlement* -- Paula Taylor   51

July, 2011--
1. *Oshkosh Air Show* -- Pamela B. Kessler   52
2. *Apparently a Case of Drunk Driving* -- Andrew Nevin   52

August, 2011--
1. *A Girl's Best Friend* -- Mart Baldwin   53
2. *The Old Gray Donkey* -- Connie Stires   54

September, 2011--
   1. *Dinnertime* -- Paula Taylor   54
   2. *A Very Modern Couple* -- Mart Baldwin   55

October, 2011--
   1. *Oracles Are Not What They Used to Be* -- Mart Baldwin   56
   2. *Going Down in Style* -- Paula Taylor   57

November, 2011--
   1. *Postmodern Homework* -- Mart Baldwin   58
   2. *The Great Reversal* -- Paula Taylor   58

   (The next three were exceptionally good—a tie for third place! So we posted all three on the Web site and are including all three in the anthology)

   3. tie for 3rd -- *Pressure* -- Adam Huddleston   59
   4. tie for 3rd -- *Cabin Fever* -- Pamela B. Kessler   60
   5. tie for 3rd -- *Maybe It's Much Too Early in the Game* -- Glenn Baldwin   60

December, 2011--
   1. *Midnight Delight* -- Paula Taylor   61
   2. *The Battle* -- Adam Huddleston   62

56 total stories for the years 2010-2011

WORD LISTS FOR WEBSITE STORIES

January, 2010—culprit, watermelon, configuration, interim, tempest

February, 2010—brace, scam, chattel, insurance, frivolous

March, 2010—dispatch, tarnished, jubilation, enzyme, materialize

April, 2010—Incorrigible, remorse, mortuary, village, paradise

May, 2010—greedy, delete, justification, ungainly, elevate

June, 2010—health, ridicule, tabulate, autonomous, strap

July, 2010—nocturne, lateral, swinish, carp, strap
   (Through an error, "strap" was included in two
   consecutive months.)

August, 2010—outmoded, mushroom, elasticity, limpid, cologne

September, 2010—respiration, indict, prestidigitator, clutch, magnet

October, 2010—situation, treaty, elusive, wreak, peaches

November, 2010—stockpot, barrel, maladroit, dividend, thermal

December, 2010—czar, complex, malady, reality, surface

January, 2011—forward, calcium, altercation, cantaloupe, stealth

February, 2011—encounter, strawberries, affiliate, repulse, swim

March, 2011—paste, fleece, exorcism, endanger, grandma

April, 2011—vulgar, brand, alleviate, cadaver, photographer

May, 2011—tantrum, intangible, bellicose, indignant, swan

June, 2011—privacy, elevator, subterfuge, derogatory, fry

July, 2011—symphony, qualm, placate, biplane, bottle

August, 2011—rebuke, segment, aversion, donkey, shine

September, 2011—transportation, opulent, assuage, microwave, product

October, 2011—session, oracle, effervescent, invigorate, precaution

November, 2011—blog, twinge, insouciant, construct, deadline

December, 2011—shortage, finesse, labyrinth, ancient, emergency

STORIES
BY THE WINNERS AND RUNNERS-UP
OF THE WEB-SITE CONTEST
FROM WWW.FLASHFICTION5.COM
2010-2011

January 2010
words: culprit, watermelon, configuration, interim, tempest

1st place--WHERE I MET MY WIFE
by Bob McGinnis

Tommy was twenty-two, his body forty-six, the configuration of a watermelon. The culprit—super-sized combos.

Tommy made a resolution--become fit at Gold's Gym. His trainer, Brandi, was a willowy blonde.

He totally fixated as she instructed warming up, moving gracefully to weights and aerobics. Even before the first workout, his heart raged as a tempest. He committed another resolution--win Brandi.

Months passed. In the interim, Tommy toned his body and relationship with Brandi. Both resolutions came to successful conclusion.

I witnessed all this from across the street at Stevens Insurance Agency, where I met my wife.

2nd place – SIMULTANEOUS RELIEF
by Daniel Venzke

In hot sunshine, children dart between adults, snatching more food from the picnic tables. In the distance, faint thunder is muted by the <u>tempest</u> of revelry.

A couple's argument over some small matter ceases when they notice their child bent over in pain. They grow increasingly concerned when his face and the sky turn matching shades of green.

In the <u>interim</u>, an angry <u>configuration</u> of dark clouds blots the sun and begins spewing rain, just as the child vomits.

Rain splashes on green <u>watermelon</u> rind, the <u>culprit</u>.

Soon, the rain is gone, and the child well.

The argument is forgotten.

February 2010
    words: brace, scam, chattel, insurance, frivolous

1st place—CHANGE OF LIFE
by Carolyn Jackson

This can't go on any longer. Somehow I need to find the courage to get past the <u>scam</u> that I have been drawn into. When we first met, I knew I had to <u>brace</u>

myself for her flamboyant and sometimes frivolous personality. After all, I did not want to be considered her chattel. What would be insurance against this sort of life? Here she comes now. I am going to take the first step and reclaim my home. This cat has ruled long enough.

2nd place—OPEN BLINDS
by Mart Baldwin

At seven, Mendel said, "He's coming at eight. Close the blinds and lock the door."

"No," Mary responded.

"Did you say 'no'?"

"Oh, Mendel, stop the scam. You can't beat the insurance . . . ."

"Well, perhaps I can't beat THEM, my lovely chattel, but I can still beat YOU!" Lunging from the wheelchair, Mendel strode across the room, fist raised.

Mary braced herself.

The front door opened. A man, video camera in hand, stood in the doorway grinning. "Thanks, Mendel. You've made it easy. We really don't like frivolous suits, you know. I always come early and peep. You'd be surprised . . . ."

March 2010
   words: dispatch, tarnished, jubilation, enzyme,
                     materialize

1st place- PROPERTY RIGHTS
by Kathleen Briske

   The emergency room was packed. Mike had been dispatched to bring in two tarnished "ladies of the night."
   Jill had claimed the corner of Main and Jubilation. It had always been Anna's corner. A catfight materialized bringing blood, tears, arrest, and a trip to ER.
   Jill kicked and screamed all the way into the exam room. Katie gave her an injection to subdue her and then cleansed her scratches and began applying enzyme cream to them.
   Jill never got a chance to say she was allergic before going into a cardiac arrest.
   Anna reclaimed her corner.

2nd place—WHAT COULD HAVE BEEN
by Joe Douglas Trent

   George stepped out on his porch, accepted the dispatch, tipped the courier, and closed the door. With trembling hands, he ripped open the envelope, but the jubilation he expected failed to materialize.

"Grant Denied," he mumbled. His baby, the <u>enzyme</u> that would mend the ravaged environment, had been spurned again.

"Unbelievable." Those government idiots had rejected him for the last time. No longer would he be their patsy, his reputation further <u>tarnished</u> with each failed application. George marched to his lab and plotted revenge.

"Wait and see what you think when Baby starts eating your precious world."

April 2010
words: incorrigible, remorse, mortuary, village, paradise

1st place--PARADISE REGAINED
by Mart Baldwin

Freudeville, a high alpine <u>village</u>, was <u>paradise</u>. Happiness and optimism pervaded; even the <u>mortuary</u> was decorated with a happy face. Then one black day, Grindel moved there. An <u>incorrigible</u>, <u>remorseless</u>, very, very long-nosed grump, Grindel snarled at little children and scattered weed seeds in everyone's garden.

What to do? No ideas. Hand-wringing despair reigned . . . , until Dr. Sigmund, a vacationing spychologist, observed: "A straightforward case.

Grindel hates his nose. You must make him proud of it."

Two months later, *Cyrano de Bergerac,* starring Grindel, began a long run at the village theatre. Freudeville, again weedless, soon regained her heavenly state.

Tie for 2nd place—HIS LOVE
by Keith Osbin

Don and I had been married thirty years when Elise was introduced to us. She had wedged her way into our paradise. Everyone talked about them in the village. Her love for him was incorrigible. When we took the trip to the big city, destiny changed for us. The wreck took Don from me. Elise was a bonus. The mortuary cremated them. Not that I'm cheap, but in remorse, I did bury them together in the same urn. Their epitaph, "My Don, a Loving Husband, and his Love, Elise, his Cat," proof that love bridges the species gap.

Tie for 2nd place—AN APPALACHIAN FAMILY
by Bob McGinnis

Billy North was second of nine siblings living in a tiny tar-papered shanty in the woods near Mountain Run. Daddy, an abusive drunk, constantly beat Momma and the kids. With no supervision,

Billy became _incorrigible_, roaming the _village_, always finding trouble.

Daddy came stomping and roaring home late one night, threatening all with a baseball bat. Momma pulled a pistol from under her apron and shot him between the eyes.

No one witnessed family _remorse_ at the _mortuary_. No _paradise_ for Daddy . . . or likely for Momma. But overnight William changed to a gentlemanly head of house and a model citizen.

May 2010
words: greedy, delete, justification, ungainly, elevate

1st place—SHE IS THE TOP OF THE BOTTOM
by Keith Osbin

You heard of the crooked man who walked the crooked mile? Well, what about the _ungainly_ lass with the _greedy_ smile? She worked only to _elevate_ her status and _justify_ her need. She fought her way to the top with a simple deed. When her coworkers weren't looking, she would lean over and type one key. A simple stroke of genius, to secure her status at the firm--never to notice it was her raise that she _deleted_ this day.

Tie for 2nd place--EVEN GOOD FRIENDS CAN BE MEAN
by Mart Baldwin

June scowled at the spiteful mirror, sighed, and deleted Chapter 4. Later her best friend, Sally, bounced in and found her, head drooped, weeping.

"What in the world, June?"

"I can't write. My wonderful characters are boring, greedy, dead cardboard. And I look like an ungainly scarecrow hoping to elevate myself. There's no justification for me to write. I hate me. I QUIT!"

"Whiner! Go wash your face, then write. I won't let you stop before 'THE END.'"

"Slave driver."

"Write!"

Months later a letter arrived. "Enclosed please find . . . book contract." Grinning, June stuck her tongue out at the stupid mirror.

Tie for 2nd place—THE CLUMSY RICH PLAYBOY
by Bob McGinnis

Trey Concord was an ungainly, handsome man. And rich.

However, he seemed bent on deleting the enormous estate his grandfather had amassed in the Texas oilfields. There was no justification for his behavior. He had everything. But Trey <u>elevated</u> squandering to supreme. He cruised his yacht filled with fine women and wines to exotic ports the world over. Yet his <u>greedy</u> nature was never satiated.

Then October 13, 2012, as he pressed his Lamborghini beyond 200 kilometers on the autobahn, world markets crashed, as did our driven driver.

Trey and the Concord family fortune came to an abrupt conclusion.

June 2010

words: health, ridicule, tabulate, autonomous, strap

1st place--STUDIES SUGGEST . . . .
by Mart Baldwin

Alfred believed, deeply and explicitly, all printed <u>health</u> claims. After reading "STUDIES SUGGEST SUNFLOWER SEEDS . . . ," he began to munch them, first as snacks then as whole meals, carefully <u>tabulating</u> his daily seed intake. Friends <u>ridiculed</u>, but Alfred, <u>autonomous</u> to the point of muleheadedness, just smiled. With "STUDIES SUGGEST BLACK <u>STRAP</u> MOLASSES . . . ," he expanded his diet. With "STUDIES SUGGEST POWDERED LLAMA HOOVES . . . ," he found a local supply.

Then, sadly, some essayist's poor attempt at parody stated: "STUDIES SUGGEST LIVE SPIDERS . . . ."

Alfred survived a ghastly week. Then, happily, another essay declared: "STUDIES SUGGEST MOST HEALTH ADVICE FOR THE BIRDS . . . ."

2nd place—THE DECISION
by Bob McGinnis

Jim Bob felt like a meaningless cog in the giant wheel.

It seemed his creative ideas were always ridiculed by those above him in the bureaucracy. He yearned for the autonomous leadership opportunities a smaller operation might afford him. He unsnapped the leather binding strap of his writing folder and began to tabulate pros and cons of leaving his position. Topping the plus column was his health. If he was no longer going in circles, he'd be less stressed.

Finally, he decided. Jim Bob quit his job as carnival carousel operator and started his own concession stand outside the grounds.

JULY, 2010
words: nocturne, lateral, swinish, carp, strap

1st place—CHOPIN'S OTHER MASTERPIECE
by Mart Baldwin

Robust Ludmilla, who loved to fish, courted Freddie, a dreamy Polish lad. One day as Freddie idly watched Ludmilla <u>strap</u> on boots and begin to fish, he drifted into gentle slumber.

A strike! A fat <u>carp</u> flapped into the boat. Freddie slept on as Ludmilla admired her prize. "See the <u>lateral</u> line, Freddie. It's his nerve." She slit the fish, removed its dripping vitals, and held them up. "Hey, look, the heart's still beating."

Freddie jerked awake. A word flashed on his mind screen—<u>SWINISH</u>!

Nevertheless, much, much later, he composed his haunting but sadly forgotten <u>nocturne</u>, "The <u>Carp</u>."

2nd place-- A POSTAL WORKER'S LIFE
by Bob McGinnis

Pretty, perky Jenny endured twelve years as a U.S.P.S. employee. She longed for promotion from her job at the main post office's customer-service counter.

Her supervisor was a <u>swinish</u> pervert. Jenny considered filing a sexual harassment grievance but would rather "go postal" and <u>strap</u> his ugly ass.

She'd apply for a <u>lateral</u> move to the suburban station but knew there'd still be people carping about rising rates and long lines.

Finally, opportunity came--a position on an all-female nocturnal shift at the sorting table. No coarse male boss or whining public, but her exciting singles nightlife--history.

AUGUST, 2010
words: outmoded, mushroom, elasticity, limpid, cologne

1st place—MOUNTAIN FOLK
by Bob McGinnis

Randy Adkins was raised third generation on West Virginia welfare. His Papaw was a coal miner till he got hurt. Memaw helped meet needs selling mushroom, root, and herb remedies, but that became outmoded.

Ma mostly traded their food stamps for drugs. Pa made white lightnin' to get a dish and color television.

Randy handcrafted fishing rods that had amazing elasticity for springing trout from limpid mountain brooks. He'd also learned from Memaw how these woods yielded bloodroot, coneflower, and ginseng.

Health food came into vogue. Memaw's "ole remedies" plus cologne from Pa's alcohol blended with ginger root made Randy rich!

2nd place—LONG WAIT AT THE TEE BOX: A CONVERSATION SNIPPET
by Glenn Baldwin

"Oh, great. Waiting on slow Japanese golfers."

"You know they're Japanese?"

"No idea. Know why Japanese visit <u>outmoded</u> Pennsylvania coalmines?"

"No ethnic jokes, please."

"It's no joke. Exotic <u>mushroom</u> farm tours. OOH! Nice Drive!"

"That'll speed things up. See his shoulders? Nice <u>elasticity</u> on the backswing."

"Now next guy, three dozen practice swings. Slow again. Plus his <u>cologne</u> is putrid."

"Sorry, that's me. For 'going out' after dinner."

"Oh, please. Some stripper's gonna lose herself in your <u>limpid</u> eyes because of Obsession for Men? Smell like cash instead. Crisp twenties."

"Whatever. Pass me a beer. Criminy, Japanese golfers are slow."

SEPTEMBER, 2010

words: respiration, indict, prestidigitator, clutch, magnet

1st place--CHICKEN DELIGHT
by Cheryl Cornelius

"She's a witch! I knew it--she's a witch!" Edith's <u>respiration</u> increased with every word of the <u>indictment</u> against her Aunt Beanie. "Look, I found her book on the black arts!"

"It's just an old book on <u>prestidigitation</u>." Harvey said.

Breathlessly Edith added, "That's not all, Harvey. The entire <u>clutch</u> of eggs has disappeared. She's cast a spell."

"Edith, there's your witch. Seems she's turned herself into a chicken <u>magnet</u>." Harvey pointed to the yard and chuckled.

"Look, y'all," Aunt Beanie squealed, waving her arms in a grand gesture toward a dozen hatchlings peeping at her toes. "IT'S MAGIC!"

2nd place--DANGEROUS MAGIC
by Mart Baldwin

Rodolfo, the great <u>prestidigitator</u>, glanced at the headlines. "Campaign Against Scammers. Two <u>Indicted</u> for Fraud, Other Arrests Imminent." Sick terror <u>clutched</u> Rodolfo's heart. His <u>respiration</u> came in gasps. With trembling hands, he removed the magnet from beneath his table, then the mirrors, hidden wire, and hollow hat that were the tools of his trade. A police car arrived outside. In Rodolfo's country, a police visit often meant the black pit.

   The police chief entered, papers in hand, and stared. "Mr. Rodolfo?" He held out the papers. "We're having a party for poor children and wondered if you might . . . ?"

OCTOBER, 2010
   words: situation, treaty, elusive, wreak, peaches

1st place--IT'S HER TURN
by Bob McGinnis

Here's the situation: Dwayne has beaten Betsy constantly the past two years they've been together at The Palms trailer court. No mercy. No treaty. Again and again. "It's just a game, hon," he says snidely. And she takes it, because she loves him.

   He's always peaches and cream when anyone's around. What could she say? What can she do? Should she be elusive? Or more aggressive? Betsy plots. Finally, she has it. Dwayne will think all hell has been wreaked on him.

   It's her turn. She makes her move swiftly.

   Dwayne stares in disbelief at the chessboard. Checkmate!

2nd place--THE TRUSTED ADVISOR
by Glenn Baldwin

The mayor fretted. "Charlie, are you sure about this? We're in a bad <u>situation</u> here."

"Sir, take credit for the heretofore <u>elusive</u> solution to the harm <u>wreaked</u> on our folk by obesity."

Shoulders squared, the mayor addressed the mob. "I hereby ban Halloween treats!"

The raging crowd threw rotten <u>peaches</u>.

"Do something, Charlie. This was your idea," hissed the mayor.

Charlie nodded and solemnly called for silence. "People, our mayor means well, but this is preposterous. I hereby declare my candidacy. Say no to his Tofu <u>Treaty</u>. Vote Charlie for Mayor!"

Approval roared.

Charlie chuckled cruelly. "Happy Halloween, Mr. Mayor."

NOVEMBER, 2010
words: stockpot, barrel, maladroit, dividend, thermal

1st place--ANOTHER CHANCE
by Bob McGinnis
Jimmy Chance grew up poor in a blighted Detroit slum. He was tiny for his age and

uncoordinated but had a heart as big as a barrel. Although others called him awkward dwarf and clumsy troll, still he shared with all. Whatever was in Momma's stockpot, Jimmy would give a dividend to hungry children next door.

As a diminutive but brilliant adult, Jimmy became a multimillionaire from the processes he created utilizing thermal energy. Using his wealth, Chance Houses were built throughout the country. The Detroit maladroit with a giving heart served millions in need, giving them another chance.

2nd place—THE FATE OF THE WORLD RESTS IN THEIR HANDS
by Glenn Baldwin

"Focus, Malagore! Destroy the barrel with your thermal beam."

"I can't. I'm too tired. And my supersuit is itchy."

"Malagore, supervillians don't whine."

Malagore stomped his foot with a petulant squeal.

"I'm NOT whining! You overfilled the barrel. Let me disintegrate a stockpot instead. And Malagore is a stupid name anyway!"

"If you don't apply yourself, you might as well be called Maladroit Man. You must vigorously prepare if you hope to defeat Captain Freedom. I guarantee HIS training is paying <u>dividends</u>, as we speak."

      Meanwhile, at the Bastion of Liberty, ...
      "Owwww! These gloves are too pinchy."
      "Focus, Captain Freedom!"

DECEMBER, 2010

words: czar, complex, malady, reality, surface

1st place—CHRISTMAS VS. THE CZAR
by Mart Baldwin

"<u>Reality</u>, Angela, is more <u>complex</u> than it appears on the <u>surface</u>," pronounced Grandfather, the family's self-appointed lifestyle <u>czar</u>. "You may not invite Bill to Christmas dinner."

"But I love him."

"Humph."

Time passed. Christmas dinner arrived, but the mood was gray. Like a dreaded <u>malady</u>, the Christmas gloomies had settled in. The doorbell rang.

"Oh," Angela said going to the door, "just another UPS . . . ."

But this "deliveryman" stepped into the room grinning. He cried, "Okay, everybody, SING! JINGLE

BELLS, JINGLE BELLS . . . ."

Soon all joined, even Grandfather, as Christmas cheer surged.

Bill, embracing Angela, exclaimed, "MERRY CHRISTMAS!" And it was.

2nd place--2084
by Glenn Baldwin

The President stormed into the Office of National Initiatives.

"I appointed you to emulate the Founding Fathers!"

"On the surface, I appear to abuse my powers, but I did your bidding. A proper Life is spent in service to the State. True Liberty is found only in service to the State. Happiness requires no Pursuit, only service to the State. My office embraces the reality of modern Life, Liberty, and Happiness. Improper freedoms only lead to complex maladies."

"I'll unmake you via Executive Order!"

"I think not. Arrest the President. Assemble the press. The people must meet their Benevolent Czar."

JANUARY, 2011
words: forward, calcium, altercation, cantaloupe,
stealth

1st place—IT ALL DEPENDS . . . .
by Paula Taylor

With <u>stealth</u>, Timmy moved <u>forward</u> through the corn stalks till he came to the low-lying <u>cantaloupe</u> vines near the barn. His goal was to cross the garden, slip into the barn, and reach the hayloft without an <u>altercation</u> with Mom over chores.

Mom was picky over things like making beds . . . even when you would just get back in them . . . and drinking milk so you got <u>calcium</u>. Moms were pains!

After sprinting through vines and into the barn, Timmy felt relief. He climbed the ladder to the hayloft. What was this . . . a soft quilt, cookies, and lemonade? Moms were great!

2nd place—RIPE FOR THE PICKING
by Pamela B. Kessler

The answering machine greeted eighteen-year-old Melanie with, "You've reached the Mellons. Please leave a message for the honeydew you're calling."

Melanie hung up. Embarrassed, she realized how <u>forward</u> she was, phoning cute, firm Jake Mellon after running into him at the health-food store. He'd been restocking the <u>calcium</u> supplements when she was distracted by a juicy <u>altercation</u> over the price of organic <u>cantaloupes</u>. With the <u>stealth</u> of a rickety truck loaded with watermelons, she'd accidentally thumped him with her shopping cart.

Later, she decided it was best to stay out of the Mellon patch, considering her given name.

FEBRUARY, 2011
words: encounter, strawberries, affiliate, repulse, swim

1st place—THE EYES OF LOVE
by Paula Taylor

To most, Valentine's Day meant <u>encounters</u> with chocolate-covered <u>strawberries</u> and things <u>affiliated</u> with romance. Agreeing, the man shuffled down the hallway, gripping the treasure in his coat pocket. He was going to see his Valentine!

Not <u>repulsed</u> by the vacant stare of the woman, his heart sang. He reached for gnarled hands and deposited the treasure . . . a pinecone, a smooth stone, a picture of a couple beneath tall pines.

Examining the objects, her head raised. Her eyes <u>swam</u> through the layers of her disease. She smiled . . . with recognition!

He gazed into her eyes of love. His world was complete!

2nd place—HOME AT LAST
by Glenn Baldwin

Captain Harrison was rotating homeward, <u>aswim</u> in memories of Kandahar.

"Patrol <u>encountered</u> an ambush. Three casualties."

"Tribal Elder Waleed upset because his daughter gave <u>strawberries</u> to Sgt. Hood. Patrol prevented Waleed from decapitating her. No casualties."

The Marine Band played and the CBS <u>affiliate</u> filmed their arrival. The captain blinked slowly. He wondered why he felt nothing. Neither Afghanistan nor home seemed real.

He was shrouded in a cocoon.

"Daddy!" Two children bolted past security and tackled Harrison in a fierce hug. All three toppled to the runway tarmac.

The cocoon shattered. Captain Harrison grinned broadly.

"I'm home at last!"

MARCH, 2011
  words: paste, fleece, exorcism, endanger, grandma

1st place—NOT MY GRANDMOTHER!
by Pamela B. Kessler

Due to a Ponzi scheme of epic proportions, even Elliott's sweet <u>grandma</u> was <u>fleeced</u>. When he discovered this, Elliott <u>pasted</u> the criminal's mug shot on his dart board and used it for target practice. This did not, however, appease his anger. He became so bitter that he eventually felt downright evil. He wanted revenge, but he knew he should leave retribution to the justice system. Still, his malicious feelings grew out of control. Therefore, in order to keep from <u>endangering</u> anyone, he sought out a qualified priest and submitted to an <u>exorcism</u>. Today, Elliott is a Walmart greeter in Cincinnati.

Tie for 2nd place—A PARTING GIFT
by Pamela B. Kessler

If anyone needed an evil spirit expelled, it was Paula. Her subordinates saved money for an <u>exorcism</u>. They felt <u>endangered</u>, yet theirs were the best-paying positions in town, so they <u>pasted</u> their lips shut and nodded at all she said. They stopped suggesting improvements because Paula would scream and send them away crying. She played no favorites and would have done the same to her own grandma. When Paula announced her retirement, they rejoiced, "Hallelujah!" They gathered their exorcism cash, bought a huge fleece blanket, put pictures of their faces on it, and hoped it would haunt her forever.

Tie for 2ⁿᵈ place—COOKIES FROM HEAVEN
by Glenn Baldwin

"Dude, your Grandma Jones is a vicious demon, reeking of the pits of hell!"

"Jason, she's just a little old lady. Crankiness and a scent like library paste aren't enough to warrant an exorcism."

"She's pulling the fleece over your eyes! She's evil."

"You mean 'wool.'"

"Wool, fleece, cotton, whatever. You're blind to her wickedness. I'm endangering my immortal soul just being here! She's the embodiment of pure . . . wait, what's that aroma?"

A frail voice called, "Boys, snack time!"

The boys dashed downstairs. Fresh cookies steamed on a plate.

"Mrs. Jones, these smell heavenly. You must be an angel!"

APRIL, 2011

words: vulgar, brand, alleviate, cadaver,
photographer

Tie for 1st place--A HAND FOR A TOOTH
by Yvonne Byrd Nunn

The yearlings bawled when the hot iron burned his brand on their rumps. Josh cringed at the smell and lit a cigar to alleviate the foul air, but still a stench lingered.

"Something's dead," he said, and started for the ravine. When he reached a plum thicket, his eye caught a flash.

Stuffed between the gnarled limbs, a decaying cadaver lay in a vulgar pose with a cubic zirconia on the left ring finger. He dialed 911.

A photographer accompanied the sheriff. In vivid color, the evening paper featured the woman clinching a dead rattle snake in her right hand.

Tie for 1st place—LANA AND JONATHAN
by Pamela B. Kessler

When Lana donned her brand-new bikini, she had the pallor of a cadaver, but, after two hours at the beach with Jonathan, she was tanned and glowing—yes, glowing because she was deeply in love. Lana adored everything about Jonathan, who eschewed vulgarity and was kind to friends, family, and strangers. She hoped Johnny would propose marriage and alleviate her yearning. She dropped hints. She waited. Finally, she hired a photographer to capture the moment when she herself would pop the question. Jonathan thought she'd never ask.

Tie for 2nd place   TRUE CRIME
by Elisha Cheeseman

Detective Swann stood frozen at the sight of the cadaver, a young man posed, as if for a photographer's lens. Before Swann could process the vulgar scene, he felt a hot breath behind him--a lifesaving warning to react to the blow before he was branded a victim.

He looked the killer in the eye, a situation only alleviated by Swann's stronger will to live.

And his gun's sound echoed in his ears as the killer fell, no longer immune to the death he spread, and closure was getting closer for the dead man's family.

Mission accomplished.

Tie for 2nd place—IN THE EYE OF THE BEHOLDER
by Glenn Baldwin

Steve groaned when the model arrived. "Thin may be glamorous, but she's <u>cadaverous</u>. Our <u>brand</u> symbolizes health. She looks ill!"

The <u>photographer's voice</u> dripped contempt as he mocked "<u>vulgar</u> American curves." "I suppose you buffoons actually want a model that smiles."

"Damn right. Pretty face, pretty body, pretty smile. You're fired! I'll shoot this campaign myself."

He turned to Sally, the lovely new intern. "Put these shoes on, you're the new poster girl for ArchAllay Therapeutic Footware, Guaranteed to <u>Alleviate</u> Foot Pain."

Stunned, Sally asked, "Don't I need wardrobe and makeup, sir?"

"No, we're only shooting from the ankles down."

MAY, 2011
words: tantrum, intangible, bellicose, indignant,
swan

1st place—SOMETIMES YOU JUST CAN'T WIN
by Don W. Bonifay

Mandy was in the midst of a full-blown tantrum. She wanted her cupcake before she ate her picnic lunch. Her indignant stance of defiance might have been humorous--but for her decision to strike out at her mommy. Mom decided to try to calm her daughter by demonstrating the intangible qualities of serenity and tranquility. She pointed to a beautiful pair of swans who were being fed bread crumbs by a little boy and his mother. As she was explaining that Mandy should emulate the peaceful nature of the swans, one of them instantly turned bellicose and attacked the other.

2nd place--NATURE'S WAY IS BEST
by Mart Baldwin

Allene and Ted, lonely thirty-somethings, loved swans. Each owned a business--Ted, SWANS INC; Allene, BLACK SWANS INC. One day, Ted, indignant, almost bellicose, appeared holding a white swan spotted with black. "Worthless! Keep your males penned, or I'll sue!"

"Well, don't have a tantrum." Allene led him to the backyard, to a pen holding white-spotted black swans. "Worthless. Your males . . . . Oh, bother, come have a cup of coffee. Let's talk."

One cup became three. Next day, Allene sampled Ted's coffee, with croissants. Soon-- <u>intangible</u> but unstoppable--love blossomed, and--lo- -a new business soon appeared: DIVERSIFIED SWANS INC.

JUNE, 2011
 words: privacy, elevator, subterfuge, derogatory, fry

1st place--DO SUPERHEROES REALLY BATTLE
TO SAVE US?
by Glenn Baldwin

The epic battle finally ended when Captain Freedom threw Malagore down an <u>elevator</u> shaft. The crowd cheered for Captain Freedom and his League of Liberty.

Freedom sneered. "Listen to those idiots. Those fools think we fought on their behalf."

"Captain, remember your policy. <u>Derogatory</u> remarks about the masses are kept strictly <u>private</u>."

"Bah! The time for <u>subterfuge</u> has passed. Now none are capable of resisting our superpowers.

All resisters will be <u>fried</u> like ants under a magnifying glass."

Freedom addressed the adoring multitudes. "A new day has dawned! You will pay tribute or suffer!"

Faces fell across all the earth.

2nd place--THE SETTLEMENT
by Paula Taylor

Cali maintained her composure until reaching the privacy of the <u>elevator</u>. She leaned against the wall of the empty cubicle, her emotion surfacing. The <u>subterfuge</u> of her ex-husband's attorney had worked. <u>Derogatory</u> statements concerning her character caused the judge to <u>fry</u> with anger and rule in favor of Bryan.

The divorce was final. Bryan received her ancestral mansion on the Mississippi. He hadn't even seen the place! She was awarded the little condo in the city.

Cali laughed uncontrollably. After all, the mansion was infested with termites and garter snakes and, because of erosion, was beginning to slide into the river!

JULY, 2011
   words: symphony, qualm, placate, biplane, bottle

1st place—OSHKOSH AIR SHOW
by Pamela B. Kessler

Geoff demonstrated the superior roll rate of his <u>biplane</u> at Oshkosh. Incredible at the controls, he artfully flew the machine as seamlessly as a maestro conducts a <u>symphony</u> orchestra. The spectators gasped when he buzzed them, but they'd no <u>qualms</u> about his skills. They applauded, hooted, and cheered him on. As if to <u>placate</u> them, he soared the plane peacefully awhile, then abruptly nose-dived onto the sidewalk. The plane shattered like a beer <u>bottle</u>.

"Awww!" they exclaimed. Obviously, it was unfixable.

They turned to Geoff, who looked up at his grandfather with big eyes. "Another 'mote-control plane, Gampa? Please?"

2nd place--APPARENTLY A CASE OF DRUNK DRIVING
by Andrew Nevin

Edward's wife had again caught him with the whiskey <u>bottle</u> he brought to all her events. While it seemed the only thing to <u>placate</u> him when forced to attend one of her soirees, it also had the effect of utterly infuriating her.

"She certainly has no qualms about making a spectacle herself," he noticed to himself while being publicly lambasted for causing a drunken scene. At the crescendo of the symphony that was her tirade, he thought, "This ought to be the most exciting thing these people see all week!"

Just then a biplane crashed through the front door.

AUGUST, 2011
words: rebuke, segment, aversion, donkey, shine

1st place--A GIRL'S BEST FRIEND
by Mart Baldwin

Barb and boyfriend Jack stopped after an hour's hard climb. Barb, unfortunately one of that population segment with aversion to all wildlife, spread their picnic. "So peaceful, sun shining, breeze . . . eeek!" A large gray animal had limped onto the scene.

"Just a donkey," Jack said in mild rebuke. "Look, a rock in her hoof." He removed the rock.

Terrified, Barb backed away but stepped into a hole. A bone cracked audibly. She screamed and fainted.

Instant panic! Then Jack loaded Barb onto the

donkey's back, and the trio descended safely.

Much later: "Jack, honey, don't forget Dolly's extra hay."

2nd place--THE OLD GRAY DONKEY
by Connie Stires

When I saw the bean field flattened and pulverized, I knew that Old Mike had been at it again! He had demolished another segment of garden just last week. I was ready to pull out my shotgun and put a shine on his backside!

Old Mike had an aversion to the rebuking last week, but I didn't think he was this vindictive! In his old age, Old Mike disregards his boundaries and wanders into forbidden paths. But the next time the old neighboring field hand pulls a stunt like this with his tractor, he'll have to pay for the damages!

SEPTEMBER, 2011
words: transportation, opulent, assuage, microwave, product

1st place—DINNERTIME
by Paula Taylor

The microwave hummed and finally beeped. The once-frozen dinner sizzled in readiness. It wasn't an <u>opulent</u> plate of beef bourguignon waiting to <u>transport</u> Walter's taste buds to culinary heaven, but it would <u>assuage</u> his immediate hunger. Closing his eyes he let the aroma capture his attention, while his mind wandered to times past when mealtime was a major <u>production</u> . . . a table surrounded by family . . . noise and laughter.

That was then. This was now. He'd eat his meal in peace without family for company. Life had moved on. But, if Walter hurried, he'd catch up with them at the mall.

2nd place--A VERY MODERN YOUNG COUPLE
by Mart Baldwin

Mary and Jimmy, starry-eyed young to-be-marrieds, were building their dream. Driving past a McMansion, Jimmy asked, "You want a house like that?"

"Oh, not so <u>opulent</u>. Three bedrooms, I think. A <u>microwave</u> and . . . ."

"I'd like four acres of lawn and, for <u>transportation</u>, a Mercedes. And some kind of robot mowing <u>product</u>."

"But what would the parents think if we lived in a place like THAT . . . ?"

"Oh, we'd <u>assuage</u> them somehow. Now for the party." They drove to Jimmy's parents' house. A uniformed man opened the car door.

"The guests are waiting in the conservatory, Mister James."

OCTOBER, 2011

words: session, oracle, effervescent, invigorate, precaution

1st place--ORACLES ARE NOT WHAT THEY USED TO BE
by Mart Baldwin

Oracles are dangerous; happy, effervescent oracles, though perhaps invigorating, are deadly. Use precaution in a session with one.

After Alice and Paul broke up, both were miserable. Alice had said: "Not yet."

Paul: "When?"

Alice: "My career . . . ." That night she cried for three hours.

Next morning, red-eyed, she entered an oracular cave. A chirpy disembodied voice said: "Your problem?"

"He proposed, and . . . ."

"Refuse him. Next."

Alice left the chamber but paused to eavesdrop. Surprise. Paul was "next."

Chirpy: "Your problem?"

"She won't . . . ."

"Good. Next."

Paul left the chamber. Alice met him. He grinned. She giggled. They embraced . . . and married that afternoon.

2nd place--GOING DOWN IN STYLE
by Paula Taylor

Clara had been depressed and unable to sleep ever since her visit to the oracle. The fortune teller had forecast physical disaster within the week. Great precaution was needed.
Walking out of the spa, Clara felt invigorated from the effervescent bath treatment and hour-long massage. Her nails were painted, her hair was curled, and her skin glowed. It was the fifth session in two days. The feeling of impending calamity had begun to fade as Clara strolled to the car, admiring her new look.
       She didn't even see the open manhole cover.

NOVEMBER, 2011
  words: blog, twinge, insouciant, construct, deadline

1st place--POSTMODERN HOMEWORK
by Mart Baldwin

Usually <u>insouciant</u>, Dexter felt a <u>twinge</u> when he read the assignment: <u>Construct</u> a blog. <u>Deadline</u> tomorrow. He frowned, then wrote:

MY <u>BLOG</u>

Neologistically speaking, English has become mush. New words are clumsy, imprecise, ugly and grammarless. Intelligent past tenses are needed. Who wants to say TEXTED? GOOGLED? TWEETED? Too many syllables, grotesque, like saying "I eated lunch" or "I thinked carefully." Instead of: "I googled Mary before she texted me, then I tweeted her back," say: "I guggle Mary before she tuxt me, then I twote her back." Smooth, crisp, euphonious . . . ."

From teacher: DEXTER, I GIVED YOU AN "F."

2nd place--THE GREAT REVERSAL
by Paula Taylor

Feeling a <u>twinge</u> of fear, James read the instructor's <u>blog</u>. The <u>assignment</u> deadline was tomorrow night. Why had he signed up for the class

in the first place? What had made him think he could
construct a website or even set up a Facebook
account for that matter? He wished he could
approach the project with the insouciant attitude of
his younger classmates. But James wasn't young. He
was sixty plus and trying to live in a thirty-something
culture. Sadly, only one embarrassing solution
remained. He'd call and beg his ten-year-old
grandkid for tutoring.

**(The next three stories were exceptionally good—
a tie for third place! So we posted all three
on the Web site and included them here.)**

Tie for 3rd place--PRESSURE
by Adam Huddleston

        Teddy sat hunched over his laptop, chewing
his lip incessantly. The deadline for his blog entry
loomed ahead of him like a death sentence. He
remembered a younger version of himself who wrote
insouciantly. That had been before the arrival of his
lovely wife.
        Teddy's wife entered his study, eliciting a
twinge of horror.
        "Yes, dear?" Teddy asked.
        "When you're finished with your little writing
project, come upstairs. My feet need massaging."
        Teddy turned to his keyboard and began
pouring his heart and soul onto the monitor. There

were more dreadful things in life than <u>blog construction</u>.

Tie for 3rd place—CABIN FEVER
by Pamela B. Kessler

As winter settled in, Rita <u>twinged</u> with regret that she was, frankly, bored. Her normally <u>insouciant</u>, light-hearted disposition had helped her weather the passing of beloved Ed, her hubby of forty-one years. Now, three years later, she sought a reason to get out of bed. Finally, inspiration! Computer savvy, she <u>constructed</u> a <u>blog</u> about her many travels, self-imposing a daily <u>deadline</u> of noon. To aid her new journey, she examined beautiful and informative postcards from faraway places, notes her friends and relatives had mailed throughout the decades. After all, no one ever said a <u>blog</u> had to be true.

Tie for 3rd place--MAYBE IT'S MUCH TOO EARLY
IN THE GAME . . . .
by Glenn Baldwin

"Our <u>deadline</u> fast approaches. Any progress, Albert?"

"None. I posted invitations, but apparently no one reads our <u>blog</u> but us."

"Well then, we must prepare for direct action. At the penultimate moment, I will dampen any <u>twinge</u> of cowardice with whiskey. Then, adopting an <u>insouciant</u> façade, I will take the nearest beautiful woman in my arms and say 'My name is Byron. Midnight approaches--prepare to be smooched!"

"A bold fantasy, Byron, but we both know it'll just be another night here in the lab."

Byron sighed. "Oh well, I'll <u>construct</u> a silicon lip-kissing simulator. Happy New Year, Albert."

DECEMBER, 2011
words: shortage, finesse, labyrinth, ancient, emergency

1st place--MIDNIGHT DELIGHT
by Paula Taylor

With <u>finesse</u>, Jennie navigated the shadowy hallway and slipped through the living room. No <u>emergency</u> had pulled her from the murky <u>labyrinth</u> of <u>ancient</u> nighttime dreams. Her problem was a miserable <u>shortage</u> of willpower. The longing for a deliciously forbidden midnight rendezvous drove her through the darkness.

Moving quietly to avoid waking her sleeping husband and children, Jennie maneuvered past the dining room. Finally, she stood in the kitchen facing the last barrier to her desire.

Jennie smiled knowingly as she swung the door open. Illuminated by the refrigerator's interior light was the leftover pepperoni pizza. Temptation had won.

2nd place—THE BATTLE
by Adam Huddleston

The bold knight stood facing his nemesis. He had spent days searching this <u>ancient labyrinth</u>, and now the beast lay before him. The time had come to settle this kingdom's <u>emergency</u>.

With a <u>finesse</u> belying his size, the knight spun through the air, swinging his sword in a wide arc. His weapon sliced through the creature's scaly flesh. The beast let out a piercing howl-- its final scream.

"Billy!" the child's mother called. "Hurry up! It's time for school!"

"Okay, mom!" Billy looked down at his diorama and grinned. He would never have a <u>shortage</u> of imagination.

TABLE OF CONTENTS
FOR STORIES BY
ORIGINAL SIX AUTHORS

WORD LISTS FOR STORIES
BY ORIGINAL 6 AUTHORS

1. thinker, geranium, bubbles, gravel, bridge

2. embedded, droopy, divinity, reminisce, foam

3. existentialism, turmoil, blackened, invasion, Surmount

4. gargle, vegetable, clip, exhaust, gossamer

5. monument, libel, grub, rainbow, ceiling

6. juxtaposition, filigree, tinker, dishwasher, hawk

7. murky, taciturn, hourglass, mushroom, alligator

8. visceral, tower, pelican, leather, latent

9. fretful, reputation, cacophony, persiflage, pepper

10. judgment, habit, listless, rhubarb, marginal

11. squish, cross, funnel, forage, grain

12. capitulate, portion, gel, zoo, suburb

13. fingernails, mountain, duck, churlish, waltz

14. livercheese, straw, mercurial, capsize, galoshes

15. port, conductor, preacher, wicker, calculate

16. cardboard, forthright, pig, scream, tone, calm

17. clatter, footsteps, strength, ivy, seclusion, fireplace

18. scarf, talisman, time, zoomed, demolish, steel

19. portrait, lemon, echo, luster, snarl

20. fork, linguini, grape, cauterize, moussaka

STORIES BY THE ORIGINAL SIX AUTHORS

#1—words: thinker, geranium, bubbles, gravel, bridge

THE PATH
by Cynthia Rios

The <u>gravel</u> path ended at a small, wooden <u>bridge</u>. We walked to the middle and looked down at the water. Harry always said I was a <u>thinker</u>, not a doer, but this time he was wrong. Too bad he wasn't here to see it.

I plucked petals off a red <u>geranium</u> that I'd carried from the funeral and threw them into the water. One by one, they floated away, taking my fears with them.

I spoke softly to the man beside me. "Only one more decision to make, honey. Should we have birdseed or <u>bubbles</u> at the wedding?"

DISRUPTION
by Frances Diane Neal

George sat on the front porch admiring the peace and beauty of his estate until his teenaged son

Clarence began playing thundering music. Suddenly, he saw a car speeding across the <u>bridge</u> leading to his drive. It sprayed <u>gravel</u>, flattened the <u>geraniums</u>, and narrowly missed his nephew, blowing <u>bubbles</u> at the edge of the lawn. George leaped from his chair to upbraid Ralph, Clarence's friend, as he stepped from the car.

"What's the matter with you, boy? Is your <u>thinker</u> busted, driving like that?"

Ralph grinned broadly, "I came over to tell Clarence I just got my driver's license."

THE PARK
by Dianne G. Sagan

The sign said "Park Closed." What could the neighborhood do to save their park? They didn't need another high-rise.

Mary remembered wandering the park with her grandmother fifty years ago. Yesterday she'd watched her own grandchildren lean over the <u>bridge</u> railing, watching the fish swim, leaving trails of <u>bubbles</u>. The <u>gravel</u> pathways crunched underfoot and made her feel young again. She recalled the potted <u>geraniums</u> arranged around *The <u>Thinker</u>* statue and late-night walks with her husband.

Neighborhood residents filed a petition, but no injunction arrived stopping what the city called progress.

GERANIUM
by Janda Raker

Vincent bred geraniums, the
latest dubbed "The Bourbon" for that area in France.
It had just sprouted, for the third April in a row.

Like *The Thinker*, Vincent sat on the
railing of the bridge. Suddenly he decided.

He grabbed a pot, poured in gravel,
covered that with loam. He tucked in tender roots,
then reached for the green plastic 7-Up bottle. On
the soil he poured the clear liquid, bubbles
burrowing their way down. He placed the dish in the
sun and stepped back, arms folded.

Perfection--a perennial "Bourbon and Seven
on the Rocks."

FAWN'S TREASURE
by Joan Sikes

Fawn stared at the bubbles in her champagne
and wished she could leave. "Too late," she
mumbled. "Here comes the thinker."

Kent pulled her to her feet. "I've got plans."

"Really? You've been thinking again."

"Yes, I have."

"Let's not walk through the garden. The geraniums make me sneeze, and the gravel gets in my sandals."

"We're not walking."

Kent guided Fawn to his car, and they drove several miles before he stopped. "See that bridge? You'll find your treasure there. Come on."

Fawn followed Kent and dug where he indicated. "A ring! Oh Kent, you think of the most wonderful things."

REVERIE
by Mary Barbara Gendusa-Yokum

Jogging in the park, Kate noticed a narrow gravel path turning toward an old bridge. Intrigued where it might lead, she found a small pond filled with green lily pads, edged with asparagus fern and geraniums. Tiny bubbles from feeding goldfish broke the surface of the water. The gentle scene was so peaceful and captivating she decided to linger awhile when suddenly she started slipping down the muddy embankment. She struggled to catch her balance.

That's when Kate saw a fellow sitting on a large boulder, lost in reverie like *The Thinker*. Wet, dirty, and embarrassed, she quickly ran away.

#2--words: embedded, droopy, divinity, reminisce,
foam

A GIRL'S BEST FRIEND
by Cynthia Rios

Rachel stood on the edge of the cliff, reminiscing about Peter and the day he had knelt in this very spot and proposed. She remembered the way his droopy moustache tickled her nose as he kissed her and handed her a small box. Rachel had opened it and found an engagement ring, embedded in a mound of divinity.

The sun glinted off the large diamond on her hand. She looked down, watching the ocean foam swirl around the white, bleached bones, on the sand, far below.

Silly Peter. He knew she preferred chocolate truffles.

BARFLY
by Frances Diane Neal

Norman seemed to be embedded in the corner stool to the bartender's left. Night after night, he occupied that space and stared into the foam in his glass of beer.

"Oh, God," he said to the world in general, "if only I didn't have to go home and face my wife's cooking." His <u>droopy</u> eyes misted over as he <u>reminisced</u> about the <u>divinity</u> his mother used to make.

In contrast, Toby, the "bar cat," sat at Norman's elbow, sublimely content, licking a paw. Too bad about these humans was his thought on the matter.

FOREVER
by Dianne G. Sagan

Alice propped her feet up, lounging against the plush pillows, munching <u>divinity</u>, her favorite candy. Sea <u>foam</u> decorated the incoming tide. She <u>reminisced</u> how she'd met Cal. His <u>droopy</u> bedroom eyes captured her heart at "hello." Alice recalled his deep voice, its resonance vibrating in her thoughts. Would he ever return from his voyage?

When twilight darkened into a star-studded sky, she saw him walking toward her. Alice ran to him and flung herself into his arms. Together at last.

Cal whispered in her hair, "I'll never leave you again." He slipped a ring <u>embedded</u> with emeralds on her finger.

DIVINITY
by Janda Raker

I love <u>divinity</u>. When Georgia and I were teenagers, her mom would fix some for slumber parties. It was perfect. Then they moved away.

Throughout the years I tried several recipes, but they were flat, failures. Finally I wrote to Georgia's mom. Despite following her directions explicitly, I produced <u>droopy</u> little mounds with pecans <u>embedded</u> in them like dirty socks peeking out of the clothes hamper.

When we were fifty, Georgia came to visit. We made divinity. We stayed up all night <u>reminiscing</u> and munching the perfect peaks of <u>foam</u>. Wonderful. Was it the cook or the company?

DROOPY'S MIRACLE
by Joan Sikes

"<u>Droopy</u>, whatcha doin'?" Sam asked.

Arthur blew the <u>foam</u> off his beer. "Nothin'." His half-closed eyes, the reason for his nickname, didn't flicker as he motioned Sam to sit.

"Remember . . . ," Sam began.

"Stop. No <u>reminiscin'</u>."

"But, Droopy . . . ."

Arthur scratched his fingernail over the fishhook <u>embedded</u> in the resin tabletop. "I'm thinkin' 'bout the future, Sam."

"What future, Droopy?"

"<u>Divinity</u> spoke to me, Sam."

Sam ducked his head and peered into Arthur's eyes. "You heard from . . . ?"

"Yep, from above." Arthur's eyes opened wide, and he gazed heavenward.

"It's a miracle," shouted Sam.

SWEET MEMORIES
by Mary Barbara Gendusa-Yokum

No matter how hard she tried, Margaret's <u>divinity</u> fudge looked like the <u>droopy</u> <u>foam</u> of men's shaving cream. She would finally give up and make fudge brownies instead.

Then one day, she found a divinity recipe in a microwave cookbook. This time she knew she would be successful. It was so easy! She <u>embedded</u> freshly cracked pecans at the last minute.

Margaret's divinity was so perfect all her friends begged for the recipe. And when her neighbors <u>reminisce</u> about their annual Fudge Cook-Off, they always say, "Margaret makes the best divinity in the world."

#3-words: existentialism, turmoil, blackened,
invasion, surmount

PHILOSOPHY 101
by Cynthia Rios

My mood <u>blackened</u> swiftly when I came
home early and found my husband, Glenn, in bed
with Ernestine. As if being fired wasn't bad enough,
now I had to deal with the <u>turmoil</u> of this domestic
<u>invasion</u> by my own flesh and blood. I wasn't sure I
had what it took to <u>surmount</u> the obstacle she had
placed before me, so I thought long and hard before
speaking.
"Does this have anything to do with that
<u>existential</u> b.s. you're always talking about, Mother?"

THE ZEALOT
by Frances Diane Neal

"Don't give me any of your namby-pamby
<u>existentialism</u>," said Jack's mother. "I watch TV. I've
seen the <u>turmoil</u> on your campus. It looked like an
<u>invasion</u> of barbarians. Your ancestors found a way
to <u>surmount</u> their difficulties without <u>blackening</u> the
family name. Leading a nude protest," she spat.
"What were you protesting? Clothes?"

"We were only trying to show how intensely we felt about our cause, Mom."

"I see. My friends and I want free breakfasts at the elementary schools. We'll go before the school board naked. I'm sure they'll get the point."

Jack swallowed hard.

OPPRESSED
by Dianne G. Sagan

The Nazi <u>invasion</u> <u>blackened</u> Samuel's homeland. Men secretly spoke of resistance but feared they couldn't escape the German oppression. Samuel fought his inner <u>turmoil</u>. Should he run or fight?

Samuel's brother Philip found work for him in a childhood friend's home. The boys grew up together in Vienna. Philip disappeared, but Samuel served his enemy by day and listened to their <u>existentialism</u> philosophy and extermination plans by night. He fed information to help <u>surmount</u> their oppressors.

Finally, the time arrived for Samuel's escape to join the resistance. They fought bravely alongside the Allies. Their victory ended five-and-a-half years of misery.

CAJUN
by Janda Raker

Discussing <u>existentialism</u> blackened Pierre's mood. "'Sides, I hates barbecue."

"I t'ink," said Jacques, "it's de man you scorn, dat competition."

"But we hafta keep our her-o-tage. Dis <u>in-vay-see-own</u> of Texans mus' be <u>sur-moun-ted</u>."

After Jacques left, Pierre's emotional turm<u>oil</u> demanded action. He created a tangle of extension cords, worn rag rugs, and timer. He moved among the checkered tablecloths, past the cash register, and out to the sidewalk. After all, the building was his and insured. Bubba only leased it.

Flames engulfed the structure, leaving a <u>blackened</u> shell. I'll rebuild, he vowed, serve gumbo, jambalaya, and catfish--Pierre's Café.

IN THE FACE OF FEAR
by Joan Sikes

The <u>turmoil</u> in the streets, fueled by the rumored <u>invasion</u>, offered an <u>insurmountable</u> obstacle. Still, Pearl had no choice. She had to reach the children before the rebels did. Anger gave wings to her feet, but, when she saw the dust-clouds in the distance, she knew they could not escape.

Pearl burst through the door and herded the children into a room, <u>blackened</u> from lack of light and mold. She shushed them, but it wasn't until she spoke that silence settled over the room. "Those crazy <u>existentialists</u> must not find us."

CHANGING VALUES
by Mary Barbara Gendusa-Yokum

The <u>turmoil</u> of the sixties and seventies <u>surmounted</u> an <u>invasion</u> of moral confusion <u>blackened</u> by voices of authority expounding <u>existentialism</u>, sensitivity training, and rejection of the establishment. Seeking freedom from societal expectations, Cliff's soul-searching found release through mind-altering substances. This rebellion contrasted sharply with his depression-surviving parents who valued conservatism and hard work. Ironically Cliff's seemingly spoiled sons, Carson and Austin, computer-literate and proactive, excel professionally, accepting the challenges of their chaotic world reminiscent of their grandparents.

Cliff still bewails his plight in denial of an increasingly technological world, living his dreams vicariously through part-time jobs and hours of television.

#4--words: clip, vegetable, gargle, gossamer, exhaust

HOWARD'S BIG MISTAKE
by Cynthia Rios

Renita admired the <u>gossamer</u> strands of the web, stretched between two rows of her <u>vegetable</u>

garden. The spider's deadly lattice had ensnared a grasshopper which struggled in vain. It reminded her of Howard, fighting to free himself from the heavily weighted fishing net she had dropped over him on their last diving excursion.

She remembered the terrified <u>gargle</u> as he began to <u>exhaust</u> the air in his tank. The end had come soon after. Sharks had followed.

The morning quiet echoed the sound of her garden shears, <u>clipping</u> her bounty. Howard should have appreciated her tomatoes properly.

WILBERFORCE STRIKES BACK
by Frances Diane Neal

Gertrude slammed a dish of hominy grits in front of her husband, Wilberforce. He made that <u>gargling</u> sound that usually preceded a complaint.

"Is this considered a vegetable or a starch?"

"Just eat it," she said in <u>clipped</u> tones. "I've got a busy day ahead, and I'm already <u>exhausted</u>. My patience is worn <u>gossamer</u> thin."

He obeyed, passive-aggressively slurping his food in a way that drove Gertrude to distraction. At last, she flushed purple and fell dead, face down on the table.

"Like the character in mythology who died of vexation," noted Wilberforce. "PMS can be murder."

TUSCAN VACATION
by Dianne G. Sagan

Ted and Grace relished their Tuscan dream vacation. The bed-and-breakfast nestled into a hillside. Italy's countryside provided the perfect backdrop for their second honeymoon.

At home, they awoke to <u>exhaust</u> and freeway noise, but not here. From the bed, they looked through <u>gossamer</u> curtains at <u>vegetable</u> gardens, vineyards, and blue skies.

Ted rolled over and gazed at Grace. He caressed her cheek, released the <u>clip</u> in her hair, and kissed her. She responded to his delicious passions. The idyllic morning was interrupted only when a breeze wafted in the open windows, bringing the sound of someone <u>gargling</u>.

SIGMUND
by Janda Raker

Sigmund's beautiful home was finished. He'd worked on it for months--plenty of living area and a nursery ready for anticipated additions to the family. No vegetables, but the pantry held many high-protein favorites.

One morning, everything changed. The woman came out, sadistically singing, in a clipped accent, "The itsy-bitsy spider . . ," and started the convertible for the first time since fall.

The engine gargled, then caught, a cloud of gray exhaust billowing from the tailpipe.

Out blew gossamer threads onto the concrete floor. Sigmund's dream home--his web--now looked like a pile of lint.

DON'T UPSET THE GREENGROCER
by Joan Sikes

Clip, clop. Clip clop. The horses' hooves kept a steady beat on the cobblestones.

A mist, as thin as a gossamer gown, spread before the greengrocer as his wagon cut a path through the fog. Charles nodded, and his chin rested on his chest. He had no more vegetables and was exhausted.

A boy darted into his path. "Mister, anything left?"

Startled, Gracie whinnied. Rosie neighed. Charles pulled on the reins. "Whoa, there, girls!"

The boy laughed. "That horse sounds like she is gargling."

Charles didn't laugh. "That's the noise she makes before she stomps on little boys."

SOUP'S ON
by Mary Barbara Gendusa-Yokum

Sally dragged herself into the kitchen. "I'm so exhausted. I don't feel like fixing supper."

She pushed up the gossamer sleeves on her dressing gown and searched the refrigerator for vegetables. As she clipped green leaves off carrots and celery, she thought, "I'll set this big pot of soup on to boil. That will give me a chance to get dressed before the kids get home from school."

"Now where did I put that glass of mouthwash? Perhaps if I gargle, my throat will feel better. Oh, no!   That wasn't chicken broth. I poured the mouthwash in the soup!"

#5--words: monument, libel, grub, rainbow, ceiling

YOUR LEASE IS UP
by Cynthia Rios

Shelly walked home in a downpour. She inhaled the earthy scent, bringing memories of fat, squirmy <u>grubs</u> that emerged with the <u>rainbow</u>. She tried not to think about the hole in her bathroom <u>ceiling</u> that was probably leaking into her tub.

Her building was a <u>monument</u> to the ravages of neglect, complete with rodents and faulty plumbing. Fear of a <u>libel</u> suit was all that kept her from running an ad in the newspaper exposing the miserly owner.

She saw a crowd outside the shabby structure.

"What happened?"

"Some slum lord fell down an elevator shaft."

"Really?"

Justice at last.

TROUBLE WITH ALGERNON
by Frances Diane Neal

Jocelyn lay staring at the <u>ceiling</u>. There must be a <u>rainbow</u> somewhere in this mess.

Really, Algernon was a <u>monument</u> to stupidity. That drunken wedding toast he made that ended in salacious remarks about the bride had landed them all in the middle of a <u>libel</u> suit. Or was it slander?

The phone rang. It was Algernon.

"Hi, Sis. How about meeting me at the Savoy for some <u>grub</u>?"

"Why?"

"I'm celebrating. Judy's father dropped the lawsuit."

"Why?"

"I found out he nobbled my dog at the Westminster dog show with a laxative so his mutt could win. Got him dead to rights."

SPRING RAINS
by Dianne G. Sagan

The Aborigines walked across the outback toward a rock impediment that stood like a <u>monument</u> over the terrain. Every year they gathered to celebrate the coming spring rains. Their sacred cave faced the sunrise.

Medicine men painted <u>rainbows</u> and animals, recording important events on the cave <u>ceiling</u> and walls. Women foraged for roots. Men killed and roasted a kangaroo over the fire for the feast. Bowls of <u>grubs</u> added to the meal.

During the dancing, a light flashed

unexpectedly. The photographic journalist ran. Later, a Sydney businessman pictured at the feast sued for libel.

THE SIGN
by Janda Raker

Leaving court, Rebecca grubbed in the bottom of her bag. Looking forward to a quiet evening at home, she dug past the stack of briefs for

the libel case and reached her Metro pass. The escalator thrust her toward the surface. She wrenched out her umbrella, looking up through the opening in the ceiling.

"A rainbow! Oh no," she groaned.

It was a sign. Her mood changed instantly. She ripped her cell phone from her bag and punched in the number. No way out. She'd be forced to take Billy--her little terror of a nephew --to the Washington Monument.

THE LAWSUIT
by Joan Sikes

Jake laughed. Hearing that song couldn't have been more timely.

"Yeah, I'm chasing <u>rainbows</u>. What's a little <u>libel</u> between friends? Besides, the hullabaloo over the scandal would die down soon. The sky's the limit," he shouted. "No <u>ceiling</u> on that! See ya later. I'm gonna get me some <u>grub</u>."

In the diner, Jake chuckled. C.J.'s accusation in that newspaper column about me and his wife havin' an affair was a big mistake. Maggie and me were too slick. No one knows, and Maggie'll never tell. Ol' C.J.'s ruined my reputation, and there's a <u>monumental</u> lawsuit comin' up.

RAINBOW DREAMS
by Mary Barbara Gendusa-Yokum

Cool breezes fluttered limp willows as Roxie walked through the Museum Garden. Just then huge raindrops pelted everywhere. She pulled her stocking cap closer. "Come on, Jackie. Let's run inside the building before the storm comes."

The entry featured a domed <u>ceiling</u> painted robin's-egg blue. Inside the foyer, a bronze <u>monument</u> dedicated to Hurricane Katrina survivors was already in place for the dedication. Roxie's commissioned painting would unveil <u>rainbow</u> hues filling the canvas sky to portray the rapture of the city rising above the <u>grubbiness</u> and <u>libel</u> of crime and corruption to promises of optimism and hope.

#6--words: juxtaposition, filigree, tinker, dishwasher, hawk

HOME IMPROVEMENT
by Cynthia Rios

"Notice the juxtaposition of the diamonds." The jeweler pointed with his pinky. "And the filigree is magnificent."

Lena picked up the bracelet and slid it around her wrist. "Ooohh, it feels wonderful, Patrick." She extended her arm, noticing the clerk was watching her like hawk. "I want it."

"How much is it?" Patrick asked.

"Six."

"Dollars?" Patrick looked hopeful.

"Hundred." The man answered with disdain.

"Forget it."

"Patrick!" Lena poked him in the ribs.

"But, what about--."

"I don't give a tinker's damn about a dishwasher, darling. You can wear gloves. Pay the man."

HOUSEKEEPING
by Frances Diane Neal

Big Mother monitored the affairs of her household like a <u>hawk</u> watching for mice. Her preference in décor was curvy elegance, so Alice's toy monkey, which was large and white, sat in <u>juxtaposition</u> to the <u>filigreed</u> living room.

Big Mother was agreeable to this encroachment on her domain but was quick to correct the insurrection of the dishwasher on the service porch. Most problems were handled by Sanford, the housecleaner and handyman.

"I'm having a man come out to look at the <u>dishwasher</u>," Big Mother announced. "I don't want Sanford <u>tinkering</u> with it." This situation called for special forces.

PUZZLED
by Dianne G. Sagan

When I arrived home, I walked into the apartment, surprised to find two men staring into my <u>dishwasher</u>. A lump of a man, <u>juxtaposed</u> next to a skinny one, appeared confused. I'd waited days for the repairmen, but on my wedding day?

I cleared my throat, and they turned to face me.

"Miss." The stick man tipped his cap.

The lump pulled up his sagging britches.

I watched them like a <u>hawk</u> as they <u>tinkered</u> with the paralyzed machine.

"I have it. We're done."

The lump pulled a plastic plate melted into <u>filigree</u> from the dishwasher bottom.

Puzzle solved.

THE TINKER
by Janda Raker

Randolph, a <u>tinker</u> mending kettles, loved Matilda, the prince's <u>dishwasher</u>.

Randolph soldered a <u>filigree</u> basket, placed it in Matilda's hand, and hurried away.

Later she carried the basket, trailing cinnamon scent, and walked into the castle. He never saw her again.

That fall, the cook said, "Matilda baked a pastry, took it in a pretty wire basket to the prince. He was taken with her and married her. An heir to the throne is expected soon."

The <u>juxtaposition</u> of bun within basket boded ill for the gentry. Randolph joined the rebellious <u>hawks</u>, overthrew and executed the entire royal family.

THE BET
by Joan Sikes

"Jed, yore our only hope. No one else could beat <u>Hawk</u>-Eye."

"I'm only a <u>tinker</u>, fellas."

Luke and Rufus pleaded, "Please. Turner bet fifty bucks against ya'."

"Yeah," Mike the <u>dishwasher</u> affirmed.

Jed contemplated the <u>filigree</u> design behind the bar. "All right."

The four men strode toward Turner and Hawk-Eye.

"Go 'head, Jed, jest try." Hawk-Eye sneered.

Jed aimed and fired six times at the juxtaposed bottles. All six exploded.
Turner set up six more.

Hawk-Eye aimed and fired. Five exploded. "Hey," he cried. "Someone hit my elbow." "There's no one standin' anywhere near ya'." Luke stepped back and grinned.

STRUCTURAL TRANSFORMATION
by Mary Barbara Gendusa-Yokum

Westin enjoyed being a <u>tinker</u>. He created beautiful <u>filigree</u> vessels in brass, copper, and tin and held patents on his electric <u>dishwasher</u>.

His favorite challenge was creating metal windmills. His eyes were as sharp as a <u>hawk's</u> as he maneuvered oiled ball bearings into <u>juxtaposition</u> within the metal ring needed for rotating the metal blades smoothly.

Westin held his breath as he tried over and over to squeeze the tiny, slippery steel balls into place. Finally his patient persistence conquered the seemingly impossible task.

Westin's satisfaction was heightened by neighborly gratitude when those flashing silvery blades forecast bad weather conditions.

#7--words: murky, taciturn, hourglass, mushroom, alligator

SPECIAL RECIPE
by Cynthia Rios

Carol stirred in the chopped <u>mushroom</u>. Frowning at the sauce's <u>murky</u> color, she added more tomatoes. She could serve <u>alligator</u>, and Frank wouldn't notice.

At dinner, she ate her salad in silence. After Frank finished, Carol cleared the table, disposed of the leftovers, and went in the bedroom to watch the latest episodes of the soap operas she taped daily. Frank belittled her shows, when he wasn't being <u>taciturn</u>.

The next day, Frank became ill. "That spaghetti had a kick. You were smart to skip it."

"Like sands through the <u>hourglass</u> . . . ."

Carol turned up the television to muffle the groans.

WILLIAM WINS
by Frances Diane Neal

William was <u>taciturn</u> by nature. He was not accustomed to flinging himself out into the dating scene, yet he had somehow managed to court and marry the beautiful Helene. What had come over him? Was it her <u>hourglass</u> figure that had caused his <u>murky</u> passions to <u>mushroom</u> out of control? He suspected he had displayed all the panache of an <u>alligator</u> clambering along a river bank after his dinner.

"Why did you marry me, Helene?" he asked one night.

"It was your ardent pursuit that won me. That and your legs, dear. They're really quite wonderful."

JUNGLE ADVENTURE
by Dianne G. Sagan

The boats skimmed along the <u>murky</u> Amazon River passing dense jungle. We sat, sweat-soaked in the bottom of the boats, slapping mosquitoes. The taciturn natives only wore shorts but appeared undisturbed and comfortable.

We continued upstream to the village where Jonathan disappeared. After three months of diplomatic phone calls, I had decided to search for him myself.

While beaching the boats, I noticed alligators sliding into the river licking their lips. A native woman with an hourglass figure stood watching, a basket of mushrooms on her hip. I couldn't believe my eyes. Jonathan stood grinning next to her.

THE PLOT
by Janda Raker

Allison noticed Jeff wasn't his usual taciturn self. He'd said they should see other people, but this morning had suggested they go picnicking. He even packed the lunch.

Jeff held Allison's hand while they looked for mushrooms and hiked to his favorite pond. They'd worn swimsuits under their clothes. He helped her remove her t-shirt, complimented her hourglass figure, then motioned for her to climb the grassy bank.

He yelled, "Last one in is a rotten egg." Just as she hit the <u>murky</u> water, she realized he remained on the bank. Then she saw the floating snout of the <u>alligator</u>.

THE LAST LOAD
by Joan Sikes

B.K. sighed. The ol' rig had lost some tread☐another <u>alligator</u> in the road.

"Time to call Jamie, B.K. That's why she gave you the <u>hourglass</u>."

B.K. raised his eyebrows. A long sentence for his <u>taciturn</u> partner.

B.K. pulled out his cell, but before he punched in the number, two trains, not ten yards from the highway, collided. Exploding tank cars spewed flames and <u>murky</u> clouds into the air. They blended into one giant <u>mushroom</u> shape, expanded, and settled onto the highway.

The last thing B.K. saw was the hourglass. The sand had run out.

THE PURPLE MUSHROOM
by Mary Barbara Gendusa-Yokum

Such a <u>taciturn</u> creature, Alicia <u>Alligator</u> floated lazily near fallen logs in her favorite corner of the <u>murky</u> Mississippi swamp as she watched the sun slowly set beyond tall cypress trees. Just then Alicia caught sight of a delicious purple <u>mushroom</u>. Its <u>hourglass</u> shape intrigued her. Whipping her tail, she propelled herself forward. Her jaws opened to clamp down on the delectable morsel. Crunch.

"Owwooo," grunted Alicia. "A thypreth knee! Get me off! I'm thuck!" Ohhh, what can I do? Push . . . push backwards . . . push hard. I'm free! Now I will keep my mouth shut.

No more mirages for me--tonight.

#8--words: visceral, tower, pelican, leather, latent

THE <u>PELICAN'S</u> BRIEFS
by Cynthia Rios

Though he'd always had a <u>latent</u> aversion to beef, his craving for fish was becoming <u>visceral</u>. His double chin seemed droopier, his pants were tighter, and his toes seemed to be growing together.

As disturbing as these changes were, he was more worried about his wife. All those long nights working on her research, in her <u>tower</u> office, were taking a toll on their relationship. But then, no one said being married to an ornithological geneticist was going to be easy.

He loosened his <u>leather</u> belt another notch. If this didn't stop, he was going to need bigger underwear.

DEUS EX MACHINA
by Frances Diane Neal

A Pelican at Blandings is English author P. G. Wodehouse's comic novel about Galahad, sprightly brother of Emsworth, the doddering lord of Blandings Castle. Galahad enjoys the busy life of London and is as out of his element in the idyllic English countryside and ivory-<u>tower</u> existence at Blandings as the Old Testament's <u>pelican</u> in the wilderness. He is considered by his bossy sisters as little better than a <u>latent</u> criminal with his dapper ways, natty clothes, and fine shoe <u>leather</u>. But he, as always, descends on the castle to outsmart his sisters and save Emsworth from their <u>visceral</u>, domineering clutches.

THE MENACE
by Dianne G. Sagan

Dorian stood contemplating the twenty towers that guarded Finlandia's borders. His visceral reaction at seeing the massive fortress brought bile up from the pit of his stomach.
He edged around the rocks, staying in the shadows, and found a secure hiding place. Dorian's fingers stroked the leather strap holding his sword. As a ranger, he had sworn no loyalty oath, but latent feelings for Marlena brought him back to Finlandia. He would save her from the Dark Lord.
Rising to face the inevitable, he startled a pelican that alerted the sentries. By morning, Dorian had met his fate beside Marlena.

PETER
by Janda Raker

Peter, atop the tower, felt bulky, awkward. Chin and feet leathery from too much sun, he swiveled, watching approaching traffic.

He'd awakened that morning knowing something was going to happen. All day he'd tried to stop the unfolding events. But it was inevitable.

Now, the reaction began in his <u>viscera</u>. A <u>latent</u> tendency was coming to fruition. He wanted to be slim as a tern, but he couldn't stop himself. He plunged from the top, aiming at the shiny spot below. He caught the sea bass in his massive pouch and gorged--a happy <u>pelican</u>, a failed dieter.

THE ATTRACTION
by Joan Sikes

Jennie's <u>visceral</u> desires overcame the now-<u>latent</u> warnings of her father. She knew Cal was no good. Then why, she wondered, was she walking as fast as the sand on the beach would allow?
A <u>pelican</u> sailed toward the waves. Would he find a juicy tidbit? Was she like that☐wanting a tidbit? The bird dove and rose, a fish flopping in his generous beak.

Jennie smiled, shaded her eyes, and looked toward the <u>tower</u>☐their meeting place. She closed her eyes and imagined him standing there in his black <u>leather</u> jacket. She broke into a run.

UNCLE LOUIE
by Mary Barbara Gendusa-Yokum

Self-centered Louie <u>Pelican</u> was lounging in his shimmering Louisiana swamp when suddenly a <u>visceral</u> response resonated from his frosty head to his <u>leathery</u> feet. He observed a cruel theft by Speckled Hawk swooping down, then making swift flight up to his perch in a tree <u>tower</u>.

Overcome with righteous indignation, Louie surprised even himself as his <u>latent</u> paternal Instinct kicked in. Hoisting his frame, he gallantly moved to rescue the tiny creature from Hawk's dinner plate.

"Jump, Freddie Frog," he called, scooping Freddie up into his beak.

Together, they whisked home, little frog chirping a serenade to his newfound uncle.

#9--words: fretful, reputation, cacophony, persiflage, pepper

AN AH-HA MOMENT
by Cynthia Rios

"A <u>fretful</u> baby can ruin one's <u>reputation</u> as a mother, you know." She frowned at the fussy infant in my arms.

"So you've told me, Mama." I could barely make myself heard over the cacophony coming from her oversized purse containing that evil-tempered, yapping ball of hair named Muffin. Fretful baby indeed.

"I thought you might want some company after that silly scare the other night, so I'm leaving Muffin with you for a few days."

Her treatment of the recent burglary took on a sense of persiflage. "Gee, thanks, Mama."

Muffin, can you say "pepper spray"?

THE BIG NOISE
by Frances Diane Neal

Leonard was fretful. He couldn't sleep for the cacophony of his sister-in-law's radio. She played music at all hours of the night. Exactly twenty-nine days ago, Felicity had come swanking in for a short

visit with Leonard and his wife Edna. The "short visit" had evolved into an indefinite stay with no end in sight. Leonard rolled over with a grunt, thinking harsh thoughts. The woman was a study in persiflage, bragging about her reputation, giving advice, changing the décor, and adding pepper to the stew. She never stopped talking. No wonder Stanley Kowalski had gone off the deep end.

THE RIVALRY
by Dianne G. Sagan

A <u>cacophony</u> erupted across the rehearsal hall. Daniel valued his <u>reputation</u> as a musician. However, his fits of <u>fretful</u> hand-waving and tripping over chair legs landed him in the percussion section. How would Daniel ever gain respect as symphony conductor?

He composed himself and walked in as dignified a manner as possible back to the podium, while David harassed him with <u>persiflage</u>. They had shared these <u>peppered</u> exchanges since childhood.

Two weeks later over dinner following Daniel's debut performance, they good-naturedly shared past escapades and future opportunities to best one another. Forever rivals--forever brothers.

CACOPHONY
by Janda Raker

James's usual hollow, guttural tone emphasized his <u>fretful</u> mood. "I want to prepare you, since you haven't attended this before."

"Why?" I asked, looking directly at him.

You'd have thought I'd thrown <u>pepper</u> in his face. He had a <u>reputation</u> for abruptness, even rudeness. But this time he really overreacted.

"You'll see. It's a <u>cacophony</u>. A thousand people verbalizing at once--pure <u>persiflage</u>!"

We strode into the convention in the Grand Plaza. Total silence. Hordes of people were gesturing. I looked questioningly at James.

"I forgot," he said. "You don't read sign language, do you?"

WILLIE AND TILLIE
by Joan Sikes

"Ah-choo. Willie, get that <u>pepper</u> away from me," Tillie demanded.

"Gesundheit," Willie tittered. "Don't be so <u>fretful</u>."

"Me? You haven't shut up since you came home. First, complaining about the tourists' noisy <u>persiflage</u>. Then about Sally's loose tongue ruining your <u>reputation</u>."

"Well, it did."

"No, it didn't."

"Those tourists. If you'd only heard the cacophony, you . . . ."

"Get another job then. Maybe in a library."

"But I like being a tour guide."

"I thought as much. Now git. I want to finish cooking in peace."

CACAKOE CACAKOE CACAKOE
by Mary Barbara Gendusa-Yokum

Carin Crowe was back in town. Her persiflage was expected to be as fretful as ever, its resounding cacophony solidifying her reputation in the neighborhood as a "hot pepper."

But the neighbors were in shock when she offered assistance to maturing fledglings with nest building. She even volunteered her services for egg-sitting when one of the parents felt too ill to provide fresh worms for its mate.

Even her voice had mellowed.

Taking the little ones under her wing, Carin organized the Bitty Bird Caroling Choir. At her fall songfest, the thrilled parents proclaimed her Birdee of the Year.

#10--words: judgment, habit, listless, rhubarb, marginal

A BITTER DECISION
by Cynthia Rios

Sister Kathleen adjusted her <u>habit</u>, preparing for supper. The garment never hung right, and the white around her face gave her complexion a <u>listless</u>, faded tone. Thank goodness final <u>judgment</u> wasn't based on attractive appearance, because hers was <u>marginal</u>.

The recurring notion that she wasn't right for this life made Kathleen uncertain. What else could she do, with no training beyond her vocation? She prayed for a sign.

As the pie was served, she bargained with God. She cut off the tip and popped it into her mouth.

<u>Rhubarb</u>.

She had her answer.

RHUBARB RULES
by Frances Diane Neal

<u>Rhubarb</u> was a finicky eater. It was his <u>habit</u> to pass <u>judgment</u> on everything set before him. He demanded excellence, and his comments were never

<u>listless</u>, but harsh and strident, when presented with food of <u>marginal</u> quality. After a long and despotic life, he was discovered by his mistress one morning, dead in bed. Tears of sadness rolled down her face during the family interment services until she visualized him bounding through cat heaven with his silken fur shimmering in the light, making sure the place came up to his expectations.

THE ADDICTION
by Dianne G. Sagan

"You promised."

"I know. My <u>judgment</u> is <u>marginal</u>, at best."

"You've got to fight this. How are you ever going to change your <u>habits</u> if you don't take responsibility for yourself?"

He gave her a <u>listless</u> look and let his gaze wander out the window behind her.

She folded her arms across her chest.

"Okay! I've lost control. I see it or smell it, and I can't say no." He sighed.

"You've got to get help. Let me do something for you," she pleaded.

"I can't stop. I have to eat the whole <u>rhubarb</u> pie."

RHUBARB
by Janda Raker

Marvin had been <u>listless</u>, for years. Every Tuesday, he ate <u>rhubarb</u> pie. Mom had cooked it weekly before he left home. Then, the university cafeteria served it on Tuesdays. In his own apartment, he learned to bake, but then discovered it frozen at Sam's.

Rhubarb was <u>marginal</u>, not his favorite. Eating it was pure <u>habit</u>.

One Tuesday, Marvin awoke with an epiphany. In that moment of sudden revelation, he perceived the scope of his freedom. He virtually ran to the supermarket where he really went out on a limb and, against his better <u>judgment</u>, bought an *apple* pie.

THE INTERROGATION
by Joan Sikes

Detective Blair slammed on his brakes and made a U-turn. "I'll go back there, even though it's a <u>marginal</u> <u>judgment</u> call."

After this second interview, Ginger was even more <u>listless</u>, although she was usually as spicy as her name. Maureen still twirled her earring, a <u>habit</u> he'd noted from the first. Blair decided neither tendency had any bearing on their guilt.

But Donald still insisted he had been working in his rhubarb patch, even though the ground was undisturbed. Blair glanced at Donald's fingernails. Abruptly, Donald shoved his hands into his pockets.

Body language spoke loudly, and Donald's shouted.

MAY'S MISSISSIPPI PIE
by Mary Barbara Gendusa-Yokum

While living in Mississippi, May learned to bake delicious rhubarb pies. She decided to enter the West Texas County Fair pie contest, but her dilemma concerned how to second-guess the judgment of her new neighbors. The culinary habit of many Southerners was to add lemon juice to the filling. She wondered if judges here would consider this as being too tart and prefer a more listless, sugary-type pie.

This decision's just too marginal so she decided to proceed according to her own taste. After all, homemakers in Mississippi are among the best pie makers in the world.

#11--words: squish, cross, funnel, forage, grain

THE OTHER SIDE
by Cindy Rios

"In order to <u>forage</u> for <u>grain</u>, you must <u>cross</u> the path," he said.

"I don't like the mud to <u>squish</u> between my toes," she replied.

"Can't be helped. It's your turn."

So she ran across quickly, looking over her shoulder as she went. Entering the field, she scooped the fallen wheat with her small hands and <u>funneled</u> it into her sack. Winter was coming, and her babies were hungry. She began to pull the heavy sack back across the road.

The cat pounced just before the mouse reached the other side. Winter was coming, and her babies were hungry.

METAPHOR AND SIMILE
by Frances Diane Neal

"Time is a <u>funnel</u>," wrote Edith. "Our lives are poured through it like <u>grain</u>."

Muriel came <u>squishing</u> through the front door, looking <u>cross</u> in her wet slippers. "It's raining so hard out there I'm soaked just going out for the paper. It's too wet to read, and I stepped in dog poop just as I spotted the cat dead in the road. By the way, you left the windows down on your car, and it's flooded."

Grim-faced, Edith continued writing, "And the black crows of trouble come <u>foraging</u> and devour the grain."

AFTER THE STORM
by Dianne G. Sagan

George barely had time to bar the shelter door when the <u>funnel</u> touched down, ripping through the farm. Rain and hail pounded golden wheat fields--<u>grain</u> beaten into the ground. Nothing escaped.

The storm wreaked havoc in a <u>crisscross</u> path through Oklahoma. The next morning under a clear blue sky, George <u>foraged</u> through the wreckage for anything to salvage. In his silent search, the only sound was the <u>squish</u>, squish of his boots in the mud. George looked at the devastation around him. Tears ran down his dirty cheeks. The bank payment came due tomorrow. All was lost.

FERDINAND
by Janda Raker

Ferdinand <u>crossed</u> the grass, entering through the open gate. He joined the group <u>funneling</u> toward the feast spread before them. For him to eat with so many others went against his <u>grain</u>, but was unavoidable. <u>Foraging</u>, he partook of first one delicacy, then another, followed by a long, cool drink.

Beginning to feel festive, Ferdie noticed the sleek good looks of young Beulah and thought of the possibilities. "What a heifer!" he thought.

However, Ferdie's interest waned at the sight of a much bigger bull approaching, cloven hooves <u>squishing</u> through the mud near the pond as he headed toward Beulah.

THE QUEST
by Joan Sikes

Wilson and Rosenbaum stooped as they entered the cave. It had taken three days of <u>crossing</u> rivers and <u>foraging </u>through thick brush to locate the opening. The pudgy Wilson <u>squished</u> through first and flipped on his flashlight. Rosenbaum followed.

An unexpected breeze swished by.

"What was that?" Rosenbaum asked.

"Air <u>funneling</u> through one of those shafts." Wilson pointed his flashlight upward. "Wow, look at that."

They struggled toward their find.

The light beam revealed a crude bowl containing a centuries-old <u>grain</u> offering.

Wilson groaned. "No jewels."

Rosenbaum wailed, "No gold."

BABY BUNTINGS
by Mary Barbara Gendusa-Yokum

Marcella was <u>crossing</u> through a pasture when she heard a tiny <u>squishing</u> sound close by. Stepping back, she saw a small bed of baby bunnies, each one wrapped close to the other, just inside a <u>funnel</u> of straw. She stepped aside so not to frighten them to run away.

Marcella heard dogs barking in the distance coming closer and closer. She ran frantically to divert their attention, but instantly they were over her.

It turned out to be a flock of wild geese returning before sundown to a nearby lake after <u>foraging</u> for <u>grain</u> all day in the fields.

#12--words: capitulate, portion, gel, zoo, suburbs

KAREN'S CRUSADE
by Cynthia Rios

"Is this tested on animals?" Karen checked the bottle.

"Probably. But they donate a <u>portion</u> of the profits to your local <u>zoo</u>."

"Not funny, Brad."

"Honey, it's hair <u>gel</u>. Don't you think you're taking this new cause of yours a little too far?"

"Bradley! I will not <u>capitulate</u> when it comes to helpless creatures."

"I like cute, furry things too, Karen. But they're just animals."

"Maybe that's true on the farm, but here in the <u>suburbs</u>, they're living beings who deserve our respect."

"Then I guess I'll return the fur coat I got you for Christmas."

"Over my dead body."

MENAGERIE
by Frances Diane Neal

Lois contemplated her <u>portion</u> in life. Her three sons, all under the age of six, tore through the living room. Alaric, who was in the lead, brandished a tube of hair gel. Percy, following after him, was known for his piercing howls. Lois covered her ears to buffer the sound. Lancelot brought up the rear waving a yardstick that had been whittled to a fine point on the end. And God knows her husband was no help.

Life in the suburbs was not what she had envisioned. She capitulated to reality—she was living in a zoo.

THE RANSOM
by Dianne G. Sagan

The two boys sported gel-spiked hair and smoked their cigarettes defiantly. They planned to kidnap KoKo, the ape, and hold her for ransom. How could two kids from the suburbs capture an ape? They put muscle relaxants in a portion of food and

threw it in the cage. As the favorite zoo animal, KoKo could bring big money if the zoo capitulated to their demands.

The boys hid in a warehouse until after hours. But, as plans can go awry, the authorities found the boys at dawn perched in a tree, holding off a rambunctious KoKo with a stick.

LEONARD
by Janda Raker

Leonard loved living in the <u>suburbs</u>--clean, restful, verdant. His <u>portion</u> of the neighborhood allowed him room to walk, watch the birds, catch a quick bite of fast food.

His usual morning routine included swimming, running laps around his oversized yard, exercising to keep his shoulders broad, and lounging in the sun.

But Leonard was resolute--he'd never <u>capitulate</u> to that <u>zookeeper</u>, especially not one with <u>gel</u> in his hair, and allow that guy to think he was boss.

To prevent the zookeeper from entering his enclosure, the culmination of Leonard's morning ritual was his loud roar.

THE CONSPIRACY
by Joan Sikes

Monica glanced in the chimp's direction and grinned. Champ mimicked her, revealing a glorious set of teeth.

"You'll be smiling even bigger in a few hours, Champ. I hope." They had left the <u>zoo</u> at noon, and once out of the <u>suburbs</u>, it wouldn't take more than an hour.

Monica sighed. Why did she always <u>capitulate</u> to Rob? "It takes time for a plan like this to <u>gel</u>," she had told him.

He'd countered, "I already have your <u>portion</u> of the stud fee. Besides, Sally's ready."

"Poor Sally," Monica mused. "And she's never even met Champ."

THE M&M DONATION
by Mary Barbara Gendusa-Yokum

Millionaire McCormick <u>capitulated</u> to the <u>suburb</u> fathers to donate a <u>portion</u> of his acreage on the northwest corner of his property to a <u>zoo</u> for exotic animals. The deal <u>gelled</u> when a deal was made to name the zoo for his beloved wife, Mamie, an advocate of animal rights.

Conflict arose when Mac's stepson Steve said he was executor of his mother's estate, and he didn't consent to the donation. In fact, he had plans to put a casino on that corner.

Mac's attorney said, "Sorry, Steve, Mac never adopted you, so you have no claim on the McCormick homestead."

#13--words: fingernails, mountain, duck, churlish, waltz

A NEW BEGINNING
by Cynthia Rios

As the bride and her father <u>waltzed</u> around the dance floor, the groom opened another bottle of champagne. He poured himself a glass and, with a silent toast, downed it in one long gulp. His <u>churlish</u> attitude and perfectly manicured <u>fingernails</u> were a strong contrast to the friendly, blue-collar ways of his new in-laws. Noticing the <u>mountain</u> of food on each plate, he doubted if they could tell the difference between their Sunday chicken and the marinated <u>duck</u>. Their lottery winnings hadn't changed them at all, he thought, but it sure will change me. He poured and drank again.

LUCKY LINDA
by Frances Diane Neal

"Got you a present, honey," Linda's husband Joe said excitedly over the phone. "I'm on my way home." He had been so <u>churlish</u> she was relieved when his friend Ralph planned a hunting trip in the mountains near Tahoe. She frowned, wondering if he'd lost money in the casinos. Soon Joe burst into the room. He waltzed over to Linda, holding a dead duck by its feet.

"Isn't he a beauty? You can clean him, and we'll eat him for supper."

Linda grabbed her handbag and headed for the door. "You fix him. I'm going to get my fingernails done."

HILL COUNTRY TRIANGLE
by Dianne G. Sagan

Lyle stood with his chin jutted out and a snarl on his lips. He hated barn-raising parties. Everyone in the mountain cove gathered to help Tom and Sarah on their new place.

Lyle stepped down off the rocks and walked straight to Sarah with a churlish expression. The waltz stopped. The couple froze. Lyle threw a duck at her feet. "I brung ya supper."

Everyone watched Lyle disappear into the woods as quickly as he'd appeared. Sarah gripped Tom's hand, her fingernails digging into his flesh.

Tom patted her hand. "It's okay. You're my woman now, not his."

THE CHURL
by Janda Raker

"Thought y'all weren't getting along."

"We weren't, but we are."

"What changed?"

"Since we moved to the <u>mountains</u>, I've been, well, <u>churlish</u>."

"So?"

"Yesterday morning, I was going to scramble eggs before Derrick went to work. Picking up the iron skillet, I broke a <u>fingernail</u>. I yelled an expletive."

"And?"

"Derrick called me a name. So I threw the skillet at him."

"Really?"

"But he <u>ducked</u>."

"Good."

"Then he walked out."

"So what happened?"

"He came home at suppertime, put on a CD, bowed, and asked me to dance. We <u>waltzed</u> around, like 'The King and I,' until bedtime."

ANDREA'S MISTAKE
by Joan Sikes

The purr of the car's motor faded as Andrea bolted the garage door and strode into the den. The magnificent view of <u>mountains</u>, purple against the twilight sky, and <u>ducks</u> peacefully gliding on the lake was now hers alone. How dare he insinuate she'd never see it again. She chuckled. "Now it's Barry who'll never see it again, and I won't have to endure his <u>churlishness</u>, nor watch him <u>waltz</u> into Tina's arms."

Andrea twisted her wedding ring. She gasped. A <u>fingernail</u> was missing. Panic overcame her when she realized where she'd lost it.

GEE, THANKS!
by Mary Barbara Gendusa-Yokum

Sparkling ripples <u>waltzed</u> into expanding circles as JennyMay's fishing lure plunked into cool, clear <u>mountain</u> waters. In just a few minutes, she felt definite tugging on her line. Excitedly, she shrieked, "I've got one!"

Racing toward her, her <u>churlish</u> friend grabbed her pole and yanked it up as hard as he could. JennyMay <u>ducked</u> as the hook and weight whipped overhead; the snarled spinning reel ripped her <u>fingernail</u> at its base. Blood poured off her finger.

"My bass! Get my bass!" she was screaming.

Her friend dropped the pole and ran off crying, "I'm sorry. I didn't mean it. Sor-r-y!"

#14--words: livercheese, straw, mercurial, capsize, galoshes

FAMILY FUN
by Cynthia Rios

I cringed as the rain pounded, and I prayed the boat wouldn't <u>capsize</u>. All weekend the weather had been like our teenaged daughter's <u>mercurial</u> temperament--changeable and unstable at best, while sometimes accelerating to volatile.

I pulled on my <u>galoshes</u> and made my way to the galley. Dreaming of tropical drinks with skinny <u>straws</u> and tiny umbrellas, I struggled to keep my balance as I prepared our meal. When I suggested to my husband we take a cruise, this wasn't what I had in mind. Tightwad.

That's okay. <u>Livercheese</u>-and-mustard sandwiches probably wasn't his idea of dinner. Bon appetit!

SHOWTIME
by Frances Diane Neal

Alice clumped up the ramp to the back porch and left her <u>galoshes</u> by the door.

"What are we having for lunch?" she asked Big Mother, taking her place at the table and picking a speck of food off the pink <u>straw</u> placemat.

"Livercheese sandwiches. Lillian Blanche and Bob are coming over this afternoon with Phillip and Bob Price."

Alice carefully pulled the fat off the livercheese. There was nothing like the mercurial relationship between Bob Price, Phillip, and Uncle Bob to capsize the usual peace and harmony around the house. It would be just like a fireworks show.

SPRING
by Dianne G. Sagan

The boys fished all day and only caught a few perch. Mama depended on them for dinner. After the long, hard winter, the thaw finally allowed them to fish and hunt again. Warm weather refreshed the family.

Papa worked clearing trees. Mama raked straw from her kitchen garden to plant vegetables. Each year brought new promise.

As the sun traveled the western sky, Sam made a mercurial pun while his brother's fishing line jerked. He burst out laughing, capsized the boat, lost his galoshes, and the day's catch.

That meant livercheese for supper. Again!

CAPSIZE
by Janda Raker

Barrett floated three days. Sun, wind, fog, helplessness. Sips of bottled water eased him.

Check the survival container. Using the blade, he broke the seal. Twenty cans of . . . livercheese. Hated the stuff, even the smell. Camille must have packed it to plague him. The last straw.

He slammed his fist on the side of the raft, but had forgotten the small knife he held. The air bladder hissed. His craft capsized and sank.

Camille always said he was mercurial. Now he'd suffer the consequences.

Perhaps I overreacted, he thought, wading ashore in his galoshes.

AN UNTIMELY TRIP
by Joan Sikes

Carl wondered why he'd given in to Walt's mercurial temperament. Now they'd have to face the music☐Patsy, that is. His galoshes were at the bottom of the river, and who knew where the canoe had gone after it capsized. On top of that, they'd lost their livercheese sandwiches.

"Here she comes. There's no hidin'," Walt said.

Patsy stormed toward them. "I could tell what happened to ya cuz I could smell y' comin'. Ya both are stayin' in the barn tonight."

At least the barn was warm, and the <u>straw</u> was dry.

ST. PATRICK'S DAY PARADE
by Mary Barbara Gendusa-Yokum

"Put on your <u>galoshes</u>, Carey, and let's hurry. The St. Patrick's River Boat Parade is always on time."

We got there just as distant church bells pealed noontime. I unwrapped my <u>livercheese</u> sandwich and placed a <u>straw</u> in my cola.

Before long we heard the exhilarating sounds of steamboat calliopes coming around the bend in the river. Passengers waved wildly. Fishing boats and skiffs trailed, bearing green Irish flags.

Suddenly a <u>mercurial</u> whistle split the air. A small boat had <u>capsized</u> in the foaming wake. Immediately, rescue teams were on the scene, while those ahead never knew what happened.

#15--words: port, conductor, preacher, wicker, calculate

COULD I INTEREST YOU IN A SANDWICH?
by Cynthia Rios

"Any port in a storm, huh, Preacher?" The conductor laughed as he punched the ticket and gestured to the last remaining spot in a railroad car full of saloon girls.

Reverend Jones just smiled as he sat down and loosened his stiffly starched collar. He tightly grasped the wicker picnic basket he had carried on board and began to calculate just how long the bags of gold dust inside would last on this week-long cross-country journey.

HOBSON'S CHOICE
by Frances Diane Neal

Preacher Jim Hobson and his wife Doris were out for a drive and got caught in a violent summer storm. Fighting hard against high winds and hail, Jim struggled manfully at the wheel, finally managing to pull the car over and stop next to the expressway support.

"I calculate we'll be safe here," said Jim. They watched as a wicker settee flew past, spotlighted by a flash of lightning. Each crack of thunder was louder and closer.

"Is concrete a conductor of electricity?" asked Doris.

"Who knows? It's any <u>port</u> in a storm, my dear," replied Jim.

THE WEDDING
by Dianne G. Sagan

Eleanor watched the tall ships in the <u>port</u> of Boston from the widow's walk of her family home. She <u>calculated</u> that her fiancé's ship should return any day. He proposed eighteen months ago and promised to marry her on his return.

Her father, the harbor master and <u>conductor</u> of ship traffic, awaited Philip's overdue ship. They carried barrels, crates, and <u>wicker</u> chests full of exotic cargo.

At last, Eleanor saw Philip's flag and sent for the <u>preacher</u>. United in marriage to his beloved Eleanor and captain of his own ship, Philip took her and sailed away with the tide.

THE CRUISE
by Janda Raker

Sunday morning, the ship headed toward <u>port</u>. On deck, the faithful attended services--text from Psalms.

Archibald listened attentively. He'd retired as Poughkeepsie Philharmonic <u>conductor</u> when his hearing deteriorated--too many tubas and timpani. But he knew he'd heard the <u>preacher's</u> every word.

Later, crewmen apprehended Archibald after he <u>calculatedly</u> threw burning matches into a stack of rattan deck furniture.

Reverend Marsh rushed to him. "Why would you do this?"

"God's wish. You said to."

"Which? What did I say?"

"Psalms 11:6 says, 'raining fire and brimstone upon the <u>wicker</u>.'"

"Not a commandment, Archibald. And it said, 'upon the wicked.'"

BELINDA'S LOVE RETURNS
by Joan Sikes

Belinda ran, her <u>wicker</u> basket swinging precariously.

The train screeched to a stop right when she'd <u>calculated</u> it would. Steam shot from beneath the engine as the <u>conductor</u> pulled the iron steps down. She caught her breath when she saw the <u>preacher</u>, the love of her life, but stopped short when she spied the lovely woman at his side.

"Belinda," he cried out. "Meet Grace, my bride. Grace, this is my best friend's sister."

"A pleasure, I'm sure." Ten-year-old Belinda curtsied, handed them the basket of <u>port</u> wine and goodies, then turned and ran, tears flowing.

CALCULATING THE COST
by Mary Barbara Gendusa-Yokum

The streetcar <u>conductor</u> was in a dilemma. Should <u>preachers</u> ride free, or should their charge be <u>calculated</u> according to distance traveled? He must make his decision before the passengers arrived from the <u>airport</u>.

He squirmed in his <u>wicker</u>-bottomed chair. "If I allow preachers to ride free, I might be accused of cheating the company. If I charge a fare, these men of the cloth may have taken a vow of poverty and have no money. If I phone my boss and ask, he'll know I haven't read our policy manual."

"To save face, I'll just pay the fares myself."

#16--words: cardboard, forthright, pig, scream, tone, calm

SAVING THE ENVIRONMENT
by Cynthia Rios

"You know how I feel about recycling. It's our responsibility." Gayla was always <u>forthright</u> about her priorities and kept her <u>tone</u> <u>calm</u>, though she wanted to <u>scream</u>.

"You really should have tried harder, George. I've explained it numerous times. Green one, glass. Blue one, plastic. Red one, paper."

She stepped over his lifeless body to put the cardboard in the appropriate container. "You always were a selfish pig, and I'm done picking up after you."

She looked at the mess on the floor and wondered which bin blood-soaked cleaning rags should go in.

A NIGHT AT THE OPERA
by Frances Diane Neal

Boris and Everard strolled along the city street, happy in each other's company. The evening had been very stressful, however.

"This is like the calm after a storm. I do wish Casper had been more forthright about the quality of his production," said Everard.

"I agree," said Boris. "The sets were cardboard, and the soprano sounded like a pig screaming."

Everard arched a brow. "She was tone deaf as well."

"The pace was hectic and uneven--most distressing."

"It looked like Halloween in an asylum."

"Yes, the costumes were impressive, weren't they?"

THE PRIZE PIG
by Dianne G. Sagan

Emma was <u>forthright</u> and committed to making her piglet a prize winner at the County Fair. He slept in a <u>cardboard</u> box by her bed at night. She worked through the spring and summer with anticipation. Papa taught her to speak in low, <u>calm tones</u> to Toby.

When the day arrived, Emma prepared Toby for the Fair. Papa heard a splash and a <u>scream</u> when she fell into the wash tub with her <u>pig</u>. Toby almost shone. She put a bright bandana around his neck for the competition.

Toby won a blue ribbon and a kiss from Emma.

POOR CHRISTMAS
by Janda Raker

Natalie smelled cinnamon rolls baking. She'd thought there wouldn't be money for even that.

On Christmas Eve, Mom had been <u>forthright</u>, talking in a <u>calm tone</u> with Natalie about finances, cutting back.

Natalie, in her robe, woke her brothers. They'd be disappointed. She hugged Mom and plugged in the lights on the little tree. Gifts were distributed, opened.

Natalie's <u>cardboard</u> package was decorated with hand-drawn poinsettias.

Opening it, she <u>screamed</u>, "The <u>pig</u>!"

Mom had gotten it at the fair when she was a girl, had kept it on her dresser. Red paint chipped, yellow flowers faded--it was beautiful.

THE CAMP VISITOR
by Joan Sikes

A <u>scream</u> destroyed the morning silence.

"What?" Jim lurched out of the tent. He shouted, "Phyllis, <u>calm</u> down." The sight of his wife chasing an animal and brandishing a <u>cardboard</u> box sent him into convulsions of laughter.

"It's not funny. Help me catch this <u>pig</u>."

"It's a javelina, Phyl." Jim grabbed her arm. "Stop! It might turn on you."

"I'm trying to catch it."

"That's not the way to get rid of it."

"It's not, huh?" Phyllis pointed toward the woods. In a proud <u>tone</u>, she announced, "He's gone. See? You have to be confident and <u>forthright</u>."

THE BUSY BODY
by Mary Barbara Gendusa-Yokum

April tried to avoid any confrontation with her boss who ordered her around until she felt she could <u>scream</u>. Mrs. Smart's accusatory <u>tone</u> never failed to take all the joy out of April's life.

"There, I heard that sound again. Give me that <u>cardboard</u> box. What are you hiding?" Mrs. Smart demanded in her abrasive, <u>forthright</u> manner. "I knew I should never trust you. Where did you get that baby?"

"From a friend" was April's <u>calm</u>, icy response. "I'm taking this <u>piglet</u> home to my niece as a surprise for her 4-H Club project."

#17--words: clatter, footsteps, strength, ivy, seclusion, fireplace

HER DELICATE CONDITION
by Cynthia Rios

The <u>ivy</u>-covered window muffled the <u>clatter</u> of <u>footsteps</u> and other sounds of life outside her unwanted <u>seclusion</u>.

She needed to regain her <u>strength</u>, they said. She needed quiet and darkness, they told her. Then she would be "well."

They were wrong. She would never be "well." Her cruel husband had seen to that with his secret "treatments." But she was smart and getting stronger. And tonight, when dear Mitchell brought her supper tray, they would see how strong.

But for now, she sat by the window, the heavy candlestick in her lap and stared through the green veil of isolation.

POOR CHARLES
by Frances Diane Neal

Charles threw the tool down with a <u>clatter</u>. "This damn <u>fireplace</u> is going to be the death of me."

He trudged to the <u>secluded</u> woodpile stacked against the garage. As he gathered logs, his strength abated. Sweat began to form on his forehead. Picking up the heavy load, he headed back to the house.

On the front porch, his <u>footsteps</u> faltered in a stray tendril of <u>ivy</u>, and he fell headlong into a decorative concrete pillar.

"Poor Charles," said his widow. "He said the fireplace would be the death of him. The English ivy on his tombstone symbolizes eternal life."

A SECRET GARDEN
by Dianne G. Sagan

Rosemary, oldest of nine children, longed for a sanctuary to find relief from her family responsibilities. One day she found a tiny garden behind ivy-covered walls. It was her secret place. She loved the seclusion, the smell of wood burning in the fireplaces, hearing her siblings' footsteps passing back and forth on the pathway. She smiled silently when they called her name.

As she grew older, the walls closed out the city clatter, and she found strength and peace behind them. At eighteen, she met Joseph--her one true love. He was the first to share Rosemary's secret garden.

NIGHT SHIFT
by Janda Raker

It had been a long night. Nicholas didn't usually work the graveyard shift, but once a year, it was necessary. He completed his final task, still in seclusion, but afraid he had a problem.

He tried to be quiet. But he bumped a pot of ivy, knocking it over and causing a terrible clatter.

Nicholas ducked into the low opening and took a <u>footstep</u> onto the closest brick. Using all his <u>strength</u>, he couldn't pull himself up. Defeated, he lowered his head, knocking off his red cap, and looked out of the <u>fireplace</u>.

Three children stared at him. Busted!

A DAY IN A DAD'S LIFE
by Joan Sikes

James stoked the blaze in the <u>fireplace</u>. He'd hoped for <u>seclusion</u> today, but Marcia had changed that plan. He sighed as he heard her <u>footsteps</u> heading toward the door.

Surprised by a loud <u>clatter</u> from the next room, he dropped the poker. The point struck his bare foot. He moaned and limped toward the noise.

"Oh no," he exclaimed. Ten-month-old Garrett sat on the floor with dirt and broken pottery scattered about. English <u>ivy</u> twirled around his head.

When he'd determined the boy had not injured himself, he laughed. "Son, you sure don't know your own <u>strength</u>."

MEAN OL' MAN
by Mary Barbara Gendusa-Yokum

Roger heard the <u>clatter</u> of Buster's old jalopy coming down the bumpy, dirt road. This time Roger was ready. With all his <u>strength</u>, he raked glowing coals from the <u>fireplace</u> onto crumpled up newspapers in the middle of the floor.

The rattletrap car rumbled to a stop. Its door slammed shut. Buster's heavy <u>footsteps</u> shuffled closer.

Scrambling out back, Roger heard the mean grouch kick in the front door, screaming and cursing.

Thick <u>ivy</u> covering the windows lent <u>seclusion</u> as Roger raced home. Buster says he'll kill anyone who comes on his property.

If his house burns, maybe he'll move.

#18--words: scarf, talisman, time, zoomed, demolish, steel

SEEK SHELTER
by Cynthia Rios

Luther considered the <u>scarf</u> a <u>talisman</u>, so when the <u>time</u> came, it was the perfect choice. The whole town grieved, wondering why his beloved Marie up and ran off like that.

Years <u>zoomed</u> by, and his secret was safe, until the tornado. Funny how a twister skips around, <u>demolishing</u> an entire <u>steel</u> structure, then leaving a small house mostly intact.

Everyone realized the skeleton hanging from the rafters was Marie, by the monogrammed piece of silk wrapped around the neck.

Poor Luther, impaled on a fence post in the yard, would never know they had finally found his errant wife.

THE OLD HOUSE
by Frances Diane Neal

Elizabeth picked at her <u>scarf</u> as she looked at the sinister house silhouetted on the hill. It had been forty years since she first saw this <u>talisman</u> of terror in 1960, but it would never be <u>demolished</u>.

People were shocked at the <u>time</u> to see Janet Leigh wearing only her underwear and astonished to see her murdered in the shower long before the movie was over. The camera <u>zoomed</u> in on her beautiful, <u>steel</u>-still face.

Was there anyone who did not know this place?

A cluster of Japanese tourists behind her tittered, pointed at the house, and whispered, "*Psycho*."

"X" MARKS THE SPOT
by Dianne G. Sagan

The pirate, Manuel Bartolomeo, wore the talisman around his neck, hidden by a red scarf. The talisman revealed an archaic map to buried gold. He knew it lay near Port Royal's harbor. Time grew short. "Weigh anchor," commanded Manuel, drawing a steel cutlass. His eyes flashed, and his teeth gleamed in a sinister smile.

They sailed the ship under a dark moon. Manuel seized the gold from under the fortress guns. As they rowed to the ship, cannon balls zoomed overhead. Boom. Splash. His ship was demolished.

Manuel clung to a floating plank, watching the gold slip into the deep.

FLASH
by Janda Raker

Her wavy, auburn tresses glinted, flowing out behind. Marva zoomed her powerful, crimson sports car down the straight, seemingly endless highway under the bright desert sunlight. The CD player poured out the Eagles' "Take It to the Limit."

Her talisman--the long silk scarf of vivid magenta and sapphire, which Carlos had bought for her when they were in Zimbabwe--streamed from her neck. Too long! The end of the fabric touched the rear wire wheel, then was sucked into its steel vortex.

The tightness was instantaneous. Demolished. Her time was up.

RAVEN'S TASK
by Joan Sikes

Raven grasped the talisman. It lay innocently in her pocket☐a small cross with the inscription "*COURAGE*." It had given her courage, all right, because finally she'd demolished the evil for all time.

Raven smiled and stepped off the curb. She had taken only two steps when a motorcycle zoomed by. Startled, she yanked the cross from her pocket and fell backward. Her skull cracked against the curb.

In searching for her identity, the paramedics discovered a bloody steel knife wrapped in a scarf. Clutched in her fist was a silver cross.

THE GOLDEN BROOCH
by Mary Barbara Gendusa-Yokum

Agnes searched under every demolished leaf and along the steel fence for the brooch Grandma had given her. Grandma always wore it on a sheer red scarf. Now it was gone. It was so special to Agnes, like a talisman transporting her to happy memories of bygone times.

Suddenly she glimpsed it straight ahead, its golden filigree glistening in the evening sunshine.

She rushed with outstretched hands to retrieve it, when unexpectedly the talisman zoomed into the air.

Mesmerized, Agnes watched as a golden swallowtail butterfly flew across the garden to sit upon petals of a brilliant red rose.

#19--words: portrait, lemon, echo, luster, snarl

HERBERT GETS A HOBBY
by Cynthia Rios

Herbert snarled as he looked at her portrait. He wasn't sure when the luster had worn off, but now thoughts of her stung like lemon on a cold sore.

Jerking open a drawer, he threw the contents into a box. Echoes of screeching demands faded . . . .

Empty the closet. Scars from biting remarks began to heal . . . .

Dig the hole . . . . Tension from demeaning insults melted away.

The neighbors speculated on Herbert's sudden gardening obsession. But when a man's wife up and disappears, what's a guy to do?

BEAUTY IS AS BEAUTY DOES
by Frances Diane Neal

At last Molly could peek inside the posh residence of the glamorous Lila Wentworth on Park Avenue. She had flowers to deliver. A uniformed maid opened the door, and Molly saw portraits lining the walls. The maid took the flowers, and as she walked to the entry table, her footsteps echoed on the marble floor. Molly could smell the lemon oil that had been used to polish the table to such a luster. Lila Wentworth stood by the staircase, the condescending snarl on her face spoiling the effect of her elegant house.

Molly thought, new money and no class.

THE VISITATION
by Dianne G. Sagan

Four generations traveled to Great-Grandpa's funeral in Florida. Family history echoed through stories about weddings, picnics, and holidays. The heirs sat together in a <u>lackluster</u> funeral home that smelled like an attic. Friends came and signed the guest book next to Grandpa's favorite <u>portrait</u> of himself by his <u>lemon</u> tree. Many gazed at the picture misty-eyed while Great-Grandma <u>snarled</u> and muttered, "I hate it."

After the burial, Great-Grandma went home to rest, but they watched in shock when she revved up the chain saw and cut down Grandpa's tree. She smiled a half-toothless smile, and peace prevailed.

SNARL
by Janda Raker

Arnold stood in the produce section, as he had most mornings, buffing apples to a high <u>luster</u>, stacking <u>lemons</u> into little pyramids. But today he kept looking up at the wall above the pharmacy counter. There was the <u>portrait</u> of his classmate, who was now the new chief pharmacist.

Arnold's mother's voice <u>echoed</u> in his head-- "Sweetheart, you must go to college. You won't be happy with a menial job."

Suddenly he freaked out, ran after an elderly lady who looked like Mom, throwing pineapples at her.

Arnold <u>snarled</u> as they took him away in the straitjacket.

TERI TAKES A STAND
by Joan Sikes

Teri had promised Mike she'd always be on time to fix his supper. Even so, he never failed to snarl his displeasure when she left for work. Today she was late, and her worst fears were confirmed when she entered the kitchen.

Flour dusted the floor, destroying its luster. Powder-coated lemons lay everywhere. The portrait, which had hung over the buffet, rested, broken, on the floor.

Teri marched into the living room and spied Mike on the recliner. Her reprimand echoed around the room. "Mike, I've had enough. Tomorrow I'm taking you to dog obedience school."

LEMON TEA AND ROSES
by Mary Barbara Gendusa-Yokum

Becky reasoned if she put lemon and honey in her cup of hot tea, her cough would go away. She curled up on her couch in a warm blanket. This was a perfect time to work on the photo album.

On a special page, Becky placed a portrait of her grandparents, decorating it with roses and gold lettering. She fixed more tea while the ink and glue dried.

Suddenly a squirt of lemon juice shot onto the photograph. Grandpa's tie looked snarled. Becky was horrified.

Then she heard his gentle voice echo, "The luster matches the lettering, Becky. That's perfect."

#20--words: fork, linguini, grape, cauterize, moussaka

FAMILY DINNER
by Cynthia Rios

"I wanted moussaka." Tony's mother-in-law shoved her plate.

"Shut up, old lady."

"Is this grape juice or piss?" She dumped the contents of her glass on the floor.

"I oughta . . . ." He raised his arm.

"Tony, she's still recuperating." Angie soothed her husband.

"Yeah, Cyclops. Thanks a lot." The old woman shook her prosthetic hook at him.

"Hey. At least I took time to cauterize it after I whacked it off. I coulda let ya bleed out." Tony lowered his head and kept eating.

"You want me to stick a fork in your other eye too?"

"Just eat your linguini, Mama."

KINDRED SPIRITS
by Frances Diane Neal

"How was your date with Felicia?" asked Boris.

"Well," replied Everard, "she was ravishing in a wine-colored dress, but you should have seen where she insisted on eating. It was a diner called The International <u>Fork</u>." He closed his eyes in distaste. "I had hoped for <u>moussaka</u>, or at least <u>linguini</u>, but . . ." He looked up at the ceiling, <u>groping</u> for words. "I chose the Welch rarebit--called rabbit at the International Fork. It positively <u>cauterized</u> the taste buds."

Boris shuddered. A quiet sympathy passed between them.

Everard smiled. "Well, ta ta," he said and went on his way, comforted.

THE FAMILY DINNER
by Dianne G. Sagan

The men always went hunting before the holiday dinner. The women stayed home, cooking and gossiping. This time on their return, instead of bringing fresh game home, they suffered scrapes and gashes on their arms from running through the woods to escape a skunk. Mama made them wash outside and then patiently tended and <u>cauterized</u> their wounds.

The rest of the women loaded the long harvest table with food and placed a <u>fork</u> by each plate. Mountains of vegetables, <u>grapes</u>, <u>moussaka</u>, and <u>linguini</u> sat steaming on the table waiting for the family to enjoy the fruits of their labors.

FXPATRIΛTF
by Janda Raker

Patricio loved <u>moussaka</u>. His Greek mother had raised him on it. But his Italian father had sent him to Rome to study. Now he loved Italy.

Dining chatter lulled him as he twined <u>linguini</u> around his <u>fork</u>. How could he tell Mama he'd never return to Athens?

Then the floor undulated, toppling wine bottles to the tile. Candles flickered, <u>grapes</u> rolled, lights dimmed. A glass shard penetrated Patricio's forearm. Electricity relit the scene. Grasping his third glass of ouzo, he applied the liquid to <u>cauterize</u> the sources of pain--his skin and his heart.

And he reconsidered his plan.

THE LAST SYMPHONY
by Joan Sikes

Sarah's <u>fork</u> made circles in her <u>linguini</u> while Mitch wolfed down his <u>moussaka</u>. His noises disgusted her. She dropped the fork and lamented that only a short while ago those sounds had seemed like a symphony to her. Now they were a dirge.

Mitch had been her one true love until he'd slashed her heart. He'd attempted to <u>cauterize</u> the wound by swearing Jill was out of his life, but the bleeding continued.

Sarah popped another <u>grape</u> into her mouth and groped for her fork. She stared at the tines and wondered, would they draw blood?

THE BUFFET
by Mary Barbara Gendusa-Yokum

Memo to Senior Assistants:

Chef Reynaldo injured his hand yesterday, requiring the wound be <u>cauterized</u>. Doctor's orders are to keep the bandages dry, so I am depending upon your excellent assistance.

Today's buffet honors our multicultural clientele. The menu includes Greek <u>moussaka</u>, Spanish tomatoes, Italian sausage <u>linguini</u>, Jerusalem stuffed dates, Jamaican sugared <u>grapes</u>, Japanese sushi, ethnic spinach salads, homemade bread, and butter.

Specialty desserts--Napoleons, chocolate éclairs, and baklava--are on the antique sideboard, accompanying the plates, <u>forks</u>, and napkins.

Please serve water, coffee, and raspberry tea.

Buffet motto: EAT UNTIL YOU ARE MISERABLE. TOMORROW YOU CAN FAST!

Sebastiani, Supervisor

THE END

GLOSSARY FOR THE WINNING WEBSITE STORIES

Definitions of the words least likely to be known by all readers.

Month of Story   Word   Definition

February, 2010—**chattel**—*n.* 1. a personal possession. 2. an item of property other than real estate.

May, 2010—**ungainly**—*adj.* (of a person or movement) awkward; clumsy.

June, 2010—**autonomous**—*adj.* (of a country or region) having self-government; acting independently or having the freedom to do so.

July, 2010—**nocturne**—*n.* 1. *Music* a short composition of a romantic or dreamy character suggestive of night, typically for piano. 2. *Art* a picture of a night scene.

July, 2010—**swinish**—*adj.* 1. like or befitting swine; hoggish. 2. brutishly coarse, gross, or sensual.

August, 2010—**limpid**—*adj.* (of a liquid) free of anything that darkens; completely clear. (of a person's eyes) unclouded; clear. (esp. of writing or music) clear and accessible or melodious.

September, 2010—**prestidigitator**—*n.* one who performs magic tricks as entertainment.

October, 2010—**wreak**—*v.t.* cause (a large amount of damage or harm.

November, 2010—**stockpot**—*n.* a pot in which stock for soup is prepared by long, slow cooking.

November, 2010—**maladroit**—*adj.* ineffective or bungling; clumsy.

May, 2011—**intangible**—*adj.* unable to be touched or grasped; not having physical presence; difficult or impossible to define or understand; vague and abstract.

May, 2011—**bellicose**—*adj.* demonstrating aggression and willingness to fight.

May, 2011—**indignant**—*adj.* feeling or showing anger or annoyance at what is perceived as unfair treatment.

June, 2011—**subterfuge**—*n.* deceit used in order to achieve one's goal; a statement or action resorted to in order to deceive.

July, 2011—**qualm**—*n.* an uneasy feeling of doubt, worry, or fear; a misgiving; a momentary faint or sick feeling.

July, 2011—**placate**--*v.t.* make (someone) less angry or hostile.

September, 2011—**opulent**—*adj.* ostentatiously rich and luxurious or lavish; wealthy.

September, 2011—**assuage**—*v.t.* make (and unpleasant feeling) less intense; satisfy (an appetite or desire.

October, 2011—**oracle**—*n.* a priest or priestess acting as a medium through whom advice or prophecy was sought from the gods in classical antiquity; a place at which such advice or prophecy was sought; a person or thing regarded as an infallible authority or guide on something.

October, 2011—**effervescent**—*adj.* (of a liquid) giving off bubbles; fizzy; *figurative* (of a person or their behavior) vivacious and enthusiastic.

November, 2011—**insouciant**—*adj.* free from concern, worry, or anxiety; carefree; nonchalant.

December, 2011—**finesse**—*n.* 1. intricate and refined delicacy; artful subtlety, typically that needed for tactful handling of a difficulty; subtle or delicate manipulation. 2. (in bridge) an attempt to win a trick with a card that is not a certain winner. 3. *v.t.* 1. do (something) in a subtle and delicate manner; slyly attempt to avoid blame or censure when dealing with (a situation or action). 2. (in bridge) play (a card that is not a certain winner) in the hope of winning a trick with it.

December, 2011—**labyrinth**—*n.* 1. a complicated irregular network or passages or paths in which it is difficult to find one's way; a maze; *figurative* an intricate and confusing arrangement. 2. *Anatomy* a complex structure in the inner ear that contains the organs of hearing and balance.

GLOSSARY
FOR THE STORIES *BY*
THE ORIGINAL SIX AUTHORS--
Definitions of the Most Esoteric Words
in this Section

Story #   Word   Definition

2. reminisce--*v.i.* indulge in enjoyable recollection of past events.

3. existentialism--*n.* a philosophical theory or approach that emphasizes the existence of the individual person as a free and responsible agent determining his or her own development through acts of the will.

3. surmount--*v.t.* **1.** overcome (a difficulty or obstacle). **2.** (usu. **be surmounted**) stand or be placed on top of.

4. gossamer--*n.* **1.** a fine, filmy substance consisting of cobwebs spun by small spiders, which is seen esp. in autumn. **2.** something extremely light, flimsy, or delicate. *adj.* **3.** made of or resembling gossamer.

5. libel--*n.* **1.** *Law* **a.** a published false statement that is damaging to a person's reputation; a written defamation. **b.** the action or crime of publishing such a statement. **c.** a false and malicious statement about a person. *v.t.* **3.** *Law* **a.** defame (someone) by publishing a libel. **b.** make a false and malicious statement about.

6. juxtaposition--*n.* **1.** an act or instance of placing close together or side by side, esp. for comparison or contrast. **2.** the state of being close together or side by side.

6. filigree--*n.* **1.** delicate ornamental work of fine silver, gold, or other metal wires, esp. lacy jewelers' work of scrolls and arabesques. **2.** anything very delicate or fanciful. *adj.* **3.** composed of or resembling filigree. *v.t.* **4.** to adorn with or form into filigree.

6. tinker--*n.* **1. a.**(esp. in former times) a person who travels from place to place mending pans, kettles, and other metal utensils as a way of making a living. **b.** a person who makes minor mechanical repairs, esp. on a variety of appliances and apparatuses, usually for a living. **c.** *Brit., chiefly derogatory.* a gypsy or other person living in an itinerant community. **2.** an act of attempting to repair something. *v.i.* **3.** to attempt to repair or improve something in a casual or desultory way, often to no useful effect. *v.t.* **4.** *Archaic* to attempt to mend (something) in such a way.

7. murky--*adj.* **1.** dark, gloomy, and cheerless. **2.** obscure or thick with mist, haze, etc., as the air. **3.** vague, confused, unclear.

7. taciturn--*adj.* (of a person) reserved or uncommunicative in speech; saying little.

8. visceral--*adj.* **1.** of or pertaining to the viscera (the internal organs in the abdomen). **2.** relating to deep inward feelings rather than to the intellect.

8. latent--*adj.* **1.** (of a quality or state) existing but not yet developed or manifest; hidden; concealed. *Biol.* **2.** (of a bud, resting stage, etc.) lying dormant or hidden until circumstances are suitable for development or manifestation. **3.** (of a disease) in which the usual symptoms are not yet manifest. **4.** (of a microorganism, esp. a virus) present in the body without causing disease, but capable of doing so at a later stage or when transmitted to another body.

9. fretful--*adj.* feeling or expressing distress or irritation.

9. cacophony--*n.* a harsh, discordant mixture of sounds.

9. persiflage--*n.* light and slightly contemptuous mockery or banter.

12. capitulate--*v.i.* to cease to resist an opponent or an unwelcome demand; to surrender.

13. churlish--*adj.* rude in a mean-spirited and surly way.

14. livercheese--*n.* a specialty food found in southern Germany, similar to bologna sausage.

14. mercurial--*adj.* **1.** (of a person) subject to sudden or unpredictable changes; (of a person) sprightly; lively. **2.** of or containing the element mercury. **3.** (**Mercurial**) of the planet Mercury. *n.* **4.** (usu. **mercurials**) a drug or other compound containing mercury.

18. talisman--*n.* an object, typically an inscribed ring or stone, that is thought to have magic powers and to bring good luck.

20. cauterize--*v.t. Medicine to* burn the skin or flesh of (a wound) with a heated instrument or caustic substance, typically to stop bleeding or prevent the wound from becoming infected.

20. moussaka--*n.* a Greek dish made of minced lamb, eggplant, and tomatoes, with cheese on top.

BIOS OF ALL THE AUTHORS—
BOTH WEBSITE CONTEST AND ORIGINAL SIX
IN ALPHABETICAL ORDER

Glenn Baldwin lives in Fox Chapel, Pennsylvania, with his wife and two children. A jack of many trades, Glenn is master of none—especially those that pay well. Before the FlashFiction5 contests, Glenn's literary exposure was limited to annual Christmas letters for family and friends. The Baldwins are rabid supporters of the Steelers. When pricked, they bleed black and gold.

Mart Baldwin, of Hendersonville, N.C., a Depression baby who grew up in the Carolinas, is a retired chemist with a Ph.D. and a year's Fulbright study in Germany. On retirement he began to write. Now, a couple of decades later, his published works include mystery novels, travel, short stories, memoirs, and essays. He and his musician wife, Betty, live in the North Carolina mountains that he rambles in and writes about. Email: Baldwins21@gmail.com

Don W. Bonifay lives in Odessa, TX. A Registered Professional Engineer and graduate of Texas A&M University, Don W. Bonifay is an Adjunct Instructor with the Texas A&M University System and an Engineering Consultant. Published in technical journals and magazines, Don is now writing creatively--a new venture, including short stories, memoirs, and a novel. He's active in church and community and enjoys reading, writing, golf, and other outdoor activities.

Kathleen (Kathy) Briske of McKinney,TX, is a retired
Registered Nurse, originally from North Dakota.
Married with four children and five grandchildren,
Kathy enjoys family, reading, traveling, bowling, golf,
and playing numerous card games with friends. Her
writing includes a column for her high school paper,
a poem for her associate-degree graduation years
ago, and many poems for going-away parties and
work-related events.

Elisha Cheeseman of Amarillo,TX, has been an
active member of Panhandle Professional Writers
since   December 2010. She has written poetry
that has been featured on Big Cat Rescue's website
(http://bigcatrescue.org/1995/poetry)and has
several short stories and two historical novels in
process, one with a paranormal-romantic twist.
Her first flash-fiction contest submission tied for
second place with one by an author who often
wins that monthly contest. She currently works
full time in customer service.

Cheryl Cornelius lives in Plainview, TX. She dabbled in flying at Miller Flying Service and spent one summer working for the FBI in Washington, D.C. She is a volunteer and board member with Hale County Literacy Council, also a member of Witness Writer's critique group, enjoys books, and writing short stories. Her favorite author is Frank Peretti.

Mary Barbara Gendusa-Yokum, native of New Orleans, lives in Texas. She specializes in inspirational writing, poetry, genealogical research, and life in the South. She has an M.Ed. in psychology, counseling, and psychometrics, with a Diplomate in Psychotherapy. Mary Barbara is listed in CambridgeWho'sWho, poetry.com, and AuthorsDen.com. She is published in *The Algerine Newsletter* by the Algiers Historical Society, New Orleans. She is one of the original *Flash Tales* authors. See www.authorsden.com/marybarbaragendusa-yokum , www.algiershistoricalsociety.org , and www.flashfiction5.com .

Adam Huddleston of Canyon, Texas is a new author with a lifetime love of reading, especially fantasy and horror. He is a retail pharmacist in Amarillo. He lives with his wife and three beautiful children. When he is not writing, he enjoys gaming and spending time with family and friends.

Carolyn Jackson lives in McKinney, Texas. Raised in Floydada, Carolyn wrote for her high-school paper, graduated, and met her husband, Carl, there. They raised two children in Lubbock, and are the grandparents of four and one grandson-in-law. Retired, Carolyn's involved with the Newcomer's Group, church, friends, and family. Two maltipoos, Daisy and Duke, bring her joy. An avid reader, Carolyn is writing her own story for the family.

Pamela B. Kessler, now of Amarillo, TX, teaches writing, reading, and mathematics in the Learning Center at Amarillo College. She has always dreamed of writing a deep, meaningful novel, but she doesn't stop reading long enough to create one. In high school, she won second prize in a poetry competition and later was a second-place winner in a short story contest. When working on a flash-fiction tale, she enjoys the art of making every word count.

Bob McGinnis of Amarillo, TX, is retired CEO of the TX and OK panhandles for the Boy Scouts of America, after a forty-year career, and continues volunteer service. He enjoys writing memoirs for family and has had stories published in newspapers, magazines, and in a book entitled *We'll Meet Again*, Amarillo College, May 2003. Bob and wife Sandi travel extensively and research family history.

Frances Diane Neal, of Amarillo, loves words, reading, and movies. She received an MA in English at WTAMU. She discovered a love for writing and writers during classes with Jodi Thomas, DeWanna Pace, and Bob Wylie. Published in *The Good Old Days* magazine and the *Beanie Baby Stories*, she has written the "Big Mother Stories," cat stories, and profiles for *Accent West* magazine, encouraged by her husband, Herschel. She is one of the original *Flash Tales* authors.

Andrew Nevin lives in Orem, Utah, with his lovely wife, Julie. He loves reading, writing, and collecting vintage axes. While he enjoys fantasy and science fiction the most, he can usually be found reading anytime two or more words are strung together on a page. Currently he works roughnecking in the oilfields of Utah and Colorado but hopes to one day write full time.

Yvonne Byrd Nunn, of Dunn, TX, is the founder/instructor of the famous "Bards of a Feather" writers. The group was formed in 1993; members reside in Johannnesburg, South Africa; Malaysia; Oklahoma, Missouri, and Texas. Monthly assignments of specific forms of poetry include critiques and a sharing of the finished poems at the end of each month. Yvonne was the Senior Poet Laureate of Texas in 2006.

Keith Osbin of Amarillo, Texas--Ten-year veteran of the U.S. Navy with Associate and Bachelor degrees in Computer Information and Business. Published poet through the International Library of Poets and member of the International Society of Poets. Featured poet in *The International Who's Who in Poetry* (2004) and *The Best Poems & Poets of 2007*. Author of Propulsion Plant Operating Sequencing Systems for the *U.S.S. Constellation* CV-64.

Janda Raker, of Amarillo, Texas, edited and co-authored this volume as well as the original *Flash Tales* and has published in *The Writer, Amarillo Style, ByLine, UltraRunning, WingWorld*, and *WTSU Review of the Arts*. A retired educator, with an MA in English, she has taught secondary through graduate school. She and her husband enjoy family, volunteering, and traveling extensively--camping, enjoying nature and big cities everywhere. See more at www.FlashFiction5.com. Get in touch through JandaRaker@gmail.com .

Cynthia (Cindy) Rios, of Amarillo, Texas, is very excited about her first publishing experience, in this anthology. She discovered her interest in writing after taking classes at Amarillo College. Cindy has been employed at Texas Tech University Health Sciences Center for over twenty years and is looking forward to retirement. She and her husband have two grown children and one grandchild and enjoy traveling on their Harley-Davidson motorcycle. She is one of the original *Flash Tales* but elected not to have stories included.

Dianne G. Sagan lives in Amarillo, Texas. Author of 18 books, Dianne G. Sagan is a recognized writer's workshop presenter. Her fiction includes a Christian fiction series on women of the Bible, *Rebekah Redeemed* and *The Fisherman's Wife;* other works include *Shelter from the Storm.* Sagan added in 2011 *Tools and Tips: What Every Writer Should Know To Go Pro.* Learn more at http://www.diannegsagan.biz. She is one of the original *Flash Tales* authors.

Joan Sikes now lives in College Station, Texas. She is a transplanted Kansan and has lived in Texas for the last 46 years. She teaches a class in memoir writing and writes a monthly column for her gated community's calendar. She has written novels, short stories, poetry and devotionals. She is one of the original *Flash Tales* authors.

Connie Stires of Youngsville, NC, majored in biology and was a master gardener. She has written four books: her personal history, her own "Big, Fat Greek Wedding," and her trips to Singapore and Cambodia. She is currently working on her travels to Thailand and her spiritual experiences. Her family is the center of her life. She also enjoys watercolors, piano, swimming, gardening, children, and animals.

Paula Taylor, a native of Oklahoma, now calls Amarillo home. A mother of three, she holds a BS in Art Education, with a minor in English, and a degree in Interior Design. She teaches private art classes and volunteers as an English teacher at the local refugee center. Her hobbies include painting, gardening, cooking, genealogy, reading, and writing.

Joe Douglas Trent--In his youth, science fiction and adventure stories fueled Joe's imagination. Education helped him see how the world works. Life gave him insight into souls touched by joy and tragedy. His first novel is *The King of Silk*, published in 2011. He lives in Lubbock, Texas, with the love of his youth, near his children and grandkids. Learn more about Joe at his website --www.jdtrent.com.

Daniel L. Venzke, known to acquaintances as Dan, lives near Midland, Texas, after residing in California, Wisconsin, Minnesota, Ohio, Alaska, and Oregon. To Dan, few things are as fulfilling as writing his stories, thoughts, and memories down for others. He has self-published several books on various subjects. Dan and wife, June, have four children and ten grandchildren.

Made in the USA
Charleston, SC
20 April 2012